Fulton Books, Inc.
Meadville, PA

Published by Fulton Books 2021

ISBN 978-1-64952-322-8 (paperback)
ISBN 978-1-64952-324-2 (hardcover)
ISBN 978-1-64952-323-5 (digital)

Printed in the United States of America

THE
CONDEMNED

A Novel by
Jesse Rosenbaum

For Mark Takacs.

Our friendship was cut short, but I am honored to have known you and am thankful for the time we shared. You inspired me, and I dedicate this book to you.

Deepest thanks and love to Dana Ziegler for supporting me, my writing, and this story. Your input and love have helped me reach this point.

Thank you to Benjamin Blake for making maple syrup and inspiring me to complete this story and get it out into the world.

Thank you also to Michael DeCicco for your feedback and support.

INTRODUCTION

My earliest memory of my love of horror was at two years old. True story. My parents had a collection of VHS tapes, and my mother told me that I would watch Stanley Kubrick's *The Shining* over and over. She figured that at my age, I didn't understand what was going on and they just let me watch it. She told me that I would finish it, rewind it, then play it again. She may have grown to regret that decision when one day when I was two or three, I put a thin yellow Wiffle ball bat through the glass in the back door, stuck my head in, and said, "Mommy, I'm home!" That was also a true story.

From there, my love of horror developed over the years and expanded into science fiction. I recalled reading *Bunnicula* by Deborah and James Howe in elementary school. Our Scholastic book fairs were a joy for me, buying books like the *Scary Stories to Tell in the Dark* by Alvin Schwartz and others like *My Teacher Is an Alien* by Bruce Coville. I would spend my middle school days in the library looking up books on vampires and ghosts. I would get lost in reading those "choose your adventure" books, but when I got to high school, something changed.

Perhaps, it was my newfound interest in girls, playing hockey or video games, but my reading dwindled, relegated only to school assignments, which I found immensely boring. Well, the Shakespeare wasn't boring. I quite enjoyed that. It really wasn't until I was nineteen that I actually wanted to buy some books that I wanted to read. The stuff I had been reading since high school and in college wasn't doing it for me. So, I started looking on the internet for books I would want to read, and I came back to my love of horror. After all, horror movies remained a staple in my life despite my diminished reading for pleasure. I still had a love for vampires, so I started looking for vampire stories.

One night, I came across a book called *I Am Legend* by Richard Matheson. I didn't know who he was, but the synopsis of the story sounded like something I would like. To my surprise, the book I purchased had that story and other short stories included in the book. To say I was addicted was an understatement. I couldn't stop reading that story. I brought it to work, to college and read it every chance I got. I was transfixed by the characters and the world that Matheson had created. I felt the anger, despair, fear, loneliness, loss, and sadness that was in Robert Neville, the protagonist. The part where he falls asleep in the cemetery and wakes up at sundown and races to get home fighting off vampires has me riveted.

A year later, I had read a lot more Matheson, and he easily became my favorite author. I loved the ability he had to write just about any genre, and he inspired me. I had decided that I wanted to try and become a writer. Now up to this point, the only writing I had down was poetry, which started as an assignment sophomore year of high school, and with some support from my English teacher, I started writing a lot of poetry. A story on the other hand felt like a challenge I wanted to take. So, over the next year or so on and off, I worked on the book you're about to read, *The Condemned*. I finished it when I was almost twenty-two, and at the time, it was a bit shorter than the version here, and it was also really out of date thematically as well as contextually in some ways.

So, why did it take me so long to finally get to this point where I could publish it? Well, in college, I met this guy, Mark Takacs, and we hit it off immediately. We became very good friends, and I learned that he wanted to be a writer too and was working on screenplays. We talked about story ideas for books, movies, and TV shows, and we would brainstorm together. We had decided that we were going to work together and make something, anything. We were each other's muses.

I remembered this one time when he came into the diner we all used to hang out at and had two pieces of paper, which he had written on front and back. He had this idea for a movie about a hit man, but not your typically hit man jumping over tables and coming out of massive gunfights unscathed. It was a fun idea, especially in our very early twenties. We planned to do a writing session at my house one day. I recalled getting ready around 10:00 or 11:00 a.m. as he was supposed to come over, but he didn't show up on time. I tried calling and texting him, but he wasn't getting back to me. I thought nothing of it and started working on the screenplay to get some ideas down so when he finally arrived, we had a lot more to work with.

Hours later, he finally called me and told me he got tied up with some family stuff and said that he was on his way. When he arrived, I told him that I was done. He apologized and said that he was sorry he was late and hoped we could still work on the screenplay, and I corrected him. I said, "No, I am done. I wrote the whole screenplay." I proceeded to read the whole screenplay, and at the end of it, Mark just loved it. He said, "Change nothing!" We were young, inspired, and felt like we could conquer the world, well the world of film anyway.

A year later, everything changed. It was April 10, 2003, and my friends and I were all getting together at the diner we went to several nights a week to hang out. We planned on ringing in Mark's twenty-second birthday at the diner and then the next night, Friday, we would all go out and do something. Well, hours passed as we all hung at the diner, but Mark didn't show up. I remembered my friend, Matt, and I stayed at the diner until about 1:00 or 2:00 a.m. when we finally went home. We had all called and sent text messages but got no response. I remembered calling Mark when I got home, and I left him a voice mail saying, "I just want to know you're okay." The next morning, Matt called me crying to tell me that Mark had been killed by a drunk driver on his way to the diner.

Our worlds were shattered. I suddenly found myself feeling all the same emotions that Robert Neville had felt in *I Am Legend*. Shortly after his funeral, my writing felt empty, incomplete. My muse was gone. Over the years, I dabbled with some writing, but there was this part of me that felt empty when I did it. I revisited this story several times over the years that followed, but I really just sat on it. I even tried writing a couple of screenplays in 2012 and 2013, but I felt equal parts sad and scared to do anything with it all and in a weird sort of way felt like doing anything with my writing without Mark to be a part of it, felt wrong in some way. I know that may sound silly, but death is a strong thing and affects us all in different ways. For me, it drowned out the fire and passion I had back in my early twenties. So, I sat on this story, but in 2019, things changed again, this time for the better.

So it was 2019, and my great friend, Ben Blake, called me one day and told me that he decided that 2019 was going to be his year of accomplishment. It's important to know that Ben had, at any given time, what felt like hundreds of ideas of things he would like to do. One such thing that he wanted to do for years was to make his own maple syrup, and dammit, he was going to do it finally. He was well underway too. He got some maple syrup, a whiskey barrel, and other items to get started. He was well on his way to accomplishing one of his long-delayed passions. I do have to say, he did finish the maple syrup, and it's fantastic.

I have to say that he inspired me. I thought to myself, *It's time to finish this story and try to do something with it.* So, from the summer of 2019 until January 2020, I worked on expanding and updating *The Condemned.* One night, I was watching TV and saw a commercial about writers getting help to find publishers for their books. That was when I got in touch with Fulton Books. Over the next five months, I worked on refining the manuscript so I could submit it for review to see if Fulton Books would want to publish it. I shared it with my friend, Michael DeCicco, to read as he and I had worked on the aforementioned screenplays back in 2012, and I respect his work. We also have a lot in common when it came to our taste for subject matter and horror as well. I also read it out loud to my fiancée, Dana, over the course of several weeks. The feedback I got from her and Michael was wonderful and really helped in refining the story.

The night of my fortieth birthday, June 27, I submitted the manuscript to Fulton Books, and a week later, they called me to tell me that they wanted to publish it! So, here we are. This story, which you are about to read, is very dear to me. It took me just about twenty years to get this story in your hands, and I truly hope you enjoy reading it as much as I did writing it. I want to thank you for taking the time to not only read this introduction but also this story.

CHAPTER 1

Saturday, April 28

Michael fell to the floor, tired and broken. Drops of blood stained his forehead as he breathed in and out erratically. Aside from his breath, he lay there motionless for a moment. His eyes lay closed as he let the cool night air pass over and through his exhausted body. He opened his eyes and took in the surrounding room in the old house. It was mostly dark and cold, but the moonbeams seemed to find their way in through the remnants of one of the windows like little beams of cold light, offering no true comfort or warmth. His back was on a dust-and-dirt-covered floor with broken boards scattered across it. He listened as the entire structure seemed to creak as the chilling wind swept through it like that of a creaking ship blowing in the wind lost at sea.

He pushed his heels into the blood-soaked wood to push his body toward the nearest wall. Exhaling and wincing, he struggled to move. His body felt like someone was standing on his chest as he tried to move. As he neared the wall, he rose himself up a little and let his back slump against the wall. He raised his shaking hands and cupped his forehead. He looked at the blood on the floor and on himself. He ran his hand through his short, dirty, and blood-spattered black hair then quickly pulled his hand back in frustration. He began to mutter to himself, "Shit…what have I done?" Tears began to form in his green eyes. "What have I done?" Michael sat there, hands trembling, thinking about what had brought him to this house in the first place. Then he remembered it all began with the dreams.

CHAPTER 2

Tuesday, April 3

Michael always loved spring semesters at college. The sun would shine most days behind white fluffy clouds and skies of blue. The energy on campus was always higher, more electric and upbeat. The winter's in the area were bitter and cold, so when the warmth came, everyone was affected by it. More of the local hotspots would open up early for the coming summer season. People would be studying outside, and the overall vibe was just better. But most importantly, it was that part of the semester where it was almost time for final exams.

It was a Tuesday, and in just about five more weeks, he would have completed his finals, have walked in his graduation commencement, and earned his bachelor's degree, a seemingly insurmountable mountain of debt from the student loan and would most likely need to still work summers at the grocery store back home. One of Michael's professors said that she could try to get him a paid internship over the summer and see if it could develop into something more, but he wasn't going to hold his breath for that. Not that he didn't think she could help, but from what he heard from other classmates, the internship was hard to get, and a bunch of people already applied for it. He was nervous about starting a job where he would actually have to put his time at university to use.

Like most people, he worried if he would do well or not. He worried if all this time here would be for nothing in that he wouldn't be able to get a job. He thought about how a cousin of his ended up not even getting a job in her area of study, which was fine for her ultimately as she was happy in her work, but it was a worry nonetheless. What would his parents say if that happened? He worried about letting them down after they had done so much for him to get to this point. Plus, he would finally be on his own once college was finished. His parents were paying for his apartment on campus, but he knew that wouldn't last. They were only doing that so he would have less of a debt to pay off from college loans. They wouldn't be able to keep paying for that apartment past graduation, and if he couldn't find a job that paid well enough, he wouldn't be able to afford rent. The thought of moving back home did not sit well with him, but that was plan C. Plan B was to rent a place with his friend, Tom, whom he met freshmen year here. Despite the uncertainty and worry, the coming change excited him. The anticipation of it all was growing in him like the days when he was young lying in bed on the night before Christmas, wondering what the morning would bring.

Michael had just finished his last class of the day and was washing his hands in the bathroom. He looked up in the mirror to check his face. He was of average build but slightly over average in height at five feet, eleven inches. Michael looked into the mirror closely to check his face but saw nothing and used his hands to fix his hair. It was a little wavy, and he debated getting it cut soon because the longer he let it get, it started to curl up on the edges, and he didn't like the way that it looked. He opened his green eyes wide and looked at them as well. He noticed the bags under his eyes from lack of quality sleep recently. The late-night studying was part of it, but for some reason he just hadn't been sleeping well. He dried his hands and walked out of the bathroom. He was starting to head back to his apartment on campus when his phone rang. He pulled the phone from his pocket and saw that it was his mom, so he tapped the answer button.

"Hi, Mom," he said.

He could tell that his mom was smiling when she spoke, "Hi, sweetheart! How you doing today?"

"I'm good, thanks, Mom. How are you? How's Dad?"

"I'm just fine. As for your father, he's okay too. He's out fiddling with that ride on lawn mower he bought himself."

"Oh, is that the used one that you told me he bought at a yard sale? Did he get that working yet?"

"Well, it was working, bless him, but it stopped about twenty minutes ago. I just wanted to check to make sure you got your check for this month. I checked. and it hadn't cleared yet."

"I'm sorry, I got it. I'll deposit it from my phone when I get back to the apartment. I need to get groceries this week anyway, so I'll remember to do it."

"Okay, sweetheart, that's good." Michael's Mom paused for a moment. "So, are you ready for your finals?"

Michael smiled. "I'm getting there. The real late-night studying starts in a couple weeks, but I feel good about my classes this semester, so I'm not that worried."

"That's good, sweetheart. Well I won't keep you. Say hi to Tom for us okay?"

"Okay, Mom. Talk to you soon."

"Okay, sweetheart, but make sure you call. I know you get distracted and are off enjoying college life, and I don't expect you to call me every day or even every week, but it's nice to hear from you aside from once a month."

"Okay, Mom. I'll call you soon, promise. Love you. Say hi to Dad for me."

"Okay, I will. Love you too, sweetheart. Bye."

"Bye, Mom."

Michael hung up the phone and headed to his apartment to deposit that check, and after that he would head out to the grocery store near campus to restock his apartment. He opened the notes app on his phone to check his grocery list to see if he forgot anything. Bread. He forgot to put bread on the list, so he typed it in. He returned his phone back to his pocket and continued on to his apartment.

Later that night, Michael awoke suddenly and shot up in his bed. His eyes flew open, and sweat dripped from his chin while his breath traveled fiercely in and out of his mouth. His torso convulsed to the rhythm of his breathing. He pivoted his arms behind himself, palms on the mattress, keeping himself up. He closed his eyes and began to breathe slowly with a fluttered rhythm in his exhale. After feeling more composed, he lay back down and just stared at the ceiling. He closed his eyes, but he couldn't return to sleep as the visions from his dreams kept flowing through his mind.

They started with Michael staring at the back of a man who stood on the floor of a canyon, which was the middle ground between the cliff that Michael stood on and a higher mountain cliff across the canyon that arched up over the canyon floor like a wave curling over about to crash. The distance between him and the other side seemed like hundreds of feet away. He couldn't recall how he knew that the figure he was staring at was a man, but he could just sense it somehow. He looked over to the cliffs and noticed that the trees that were growing straight down out of the earth on the curl of the cliff. Their roots were exposed under the earth of the curl, which had seemed to be eroding away from itself. The trees slanted left and right under the cliff, and he saw what appeared to be lines coming down out of the trees. At the end of these lines, he saw odd shapes slowly banging into one another. As he moved closer and focused in more, he could see that they appeared to be naked bodies. He walked closer still, and as he shortened the distance, he noticed something peculiar. Some of the bodies were missing limbs and some didn't even have heads. He recalled feeling frightened as he stared at the ravaged bodies that hung upside down, swaying slowly from the trees growing down from the curled cliffs above. Many hung by their necks, but a few hung by their ankles. He even saw one with no upper body, just legs cut off at the waist.

He remembered then how his focus shifted, and he started to stare at the man still standing on the middle ground in the distance. The man's back was to Michael as the man stood staring up at the cliffs. Michael then started looking out at the canyon floor, watching the back and forth movement of what appeared to be a variety of light to dark sphere-like shapes. He could swear that he heard the voices of what seemed to be hundreds of people screaming from the canyon floor, but he could see no one. He remembered then how now he was watching himself as if removed from his own body listening to that sound. It was then that he realized that the man on the canyon floor was him. In a flash, he was now standing on the canyon floor. He stood there listening to the sound of people crying, cursing, and screaming. Some were muffled and others were rather loud. He listened as the sounds echoed off the canyon walls. The echoes started to grow louder, and they swirled around him.

Standing on the canyon floor, his vision focused, and he could see exactly where the sound was coming from. All around him, he saw people who were buried up to their necks in the soil screaming as ants, scorpions, centipedes, and other insects crawled upon them eating and stinging their flesh, traveling in and out of the ears, mouths, and noses. Across the canyon floor, there were pools of blood on the heads and ground below the high-curled cliff from the ravaged bodies hanging from the descending trees above. Then his attention was refocused as he heard a clear voice, one without the sounds of suffering, without the sounds of pain. As he turned his head toward the right, he saw a dark figure. It stood solemnly, and even though the area was illuminated, the light seemed to miss this dark figure. Michael could not make out any type of definition on its body. It seemed almost like a shadow just standing there, waving to him as if it wanted Michael to come closer.

Michael began to move forward, but then he looked up and saw what he could only rationalize as demons. The kind he had seen in comic books or cheap horror films. That was the only possible explanation he could tell himself. Their misshapen forms, some with horns, many with jagged, sharp teeth. Some had wings like that of a bat or dragon while others had insect-like wings, like a dragonfly. Their wet, leathery skin were the colors of the earth, dirt and clay. He could sense the loneliness, fear, and rage emanating from them. He watched as the winged ones and even other demons with no wings above the canyon floor floated along the breeze.

Looking back down at ground level, he could now see that there were other demons walking along the canyon floor. Some had the bodies of screaming people on their shoulders. The demons were carrying those people off into the distance, like bags of mulch. He began to move closer to the dark figure, but then he was knocked down by a demon that looked as if he had been burned in a chemical fire. Its skin was all together blistering, appeared to be melting and oozing puss in some places. There were sores all over its body with large scarred welts across its chest and abdomen. Michael stared as the demon continued to walk as if unaffected by the collision. It was then that Michael noticed the demon's arms or the lack thereof. There were stitches and scars around the demon's armpits. It seemed as if its arms had been removed and replaced with something inhuman, something unnatural. If he had to describe it, it seemed like charred tree branches. Something Michael had never seen or could comprehend. It was then that he awoke so suddenly.

Even now that he was awake, that clear voice kept running through his mind. "I shall become of your world," it said. The dark figure's voice sounded almost angelic. Michael recalled how when hearing that voice, the tone seemed to put Michael at ease, but it was what was said that filled him with confusion, and now for some reason, that ease he felt was vanishing as he felt a sense of fear replacing it. Who or what was this figure in his dreams and where was that awful place? He remembered his friend, Jeanie, telling him about how dreams were sometimes a reflection of how one might be feeling or perhaps a glimpse of what's to come in one's own life. Michael thought to himself, *Perhaps that's all it is.* But a part of Michael felt that was too simple of an answer. He got up to get a bottle of water and drained half the bottle in what felt like no time at all. He returned to bed where he lay awake tossing and turning for about an hour before he drifted off back to sleep.

CHAPTER 3

Wednesday, April 4

At 9:30 a.m., Michael woke up to the sound of his alarm clock radio. He liked to set the volume all the way up so that it would be so loud he knew that he would wake up. He knew that he could use his phone as an alarm, but he liked waking up to the music of the radio. He even put the clock on the far side of the room so he would have to get out of bed to turn it off. Some mornings, he cursed himself for putting it so far away from the bed, and today was no exception. Still, he rolled himself out of bed, walked over to the alarm clock, and turned down the volume. He walked back to the bed and fell backward on to it. He lay there for a few minutes, staring up at the ceiling, listening to the music. Then he sat up and reached for the bottle of water he had placed at his bedside the night before and finished its contents.

Placing the bottle back down, he stood up out of bed then got a pair of jeans, underwear, socks, and a T-shirt out of his drawers. Then he headed toward the bathroom to start his morning routine of brushing his teeth and showing. He checked his face in the mirror and decided that he didn't need a shave today.

At the rate his facial hair had grown, he generally needed to shave once per week. *Perhaps in two more days*, he thought. After a shower, Michael got dressed as quickly as he could, grabbed his things and then hurried out the door as he didn't want to be late for his first class of the day, business law.

After class, he went to the cafeteria for a small lunch with his friend, Tom. Michael sat alone staring blankly at his cup of coffee with the visions of the dream running through his mind over and over again, and that figure, just thinking of it made Michael's heart race faster. Michael focused on his cup of coffee and noticed that his hand was shaking slightly. He heard a voice.

"Man, that McVicker is insane!" Tom said as he shook his head. Michael refocused his attention as Tom sat down. "How does he expect us to remember all these statutes by next class?"

Michael sipped his coffee then looked at Tom. "I don't know, but I know what I am doing tonight."

They looked at each other, paused, and then said in unison, "Studying!" They nodded in agreement and laughed.

Tom began to talk about the chapter concerning the Uniform Commercial Code, but his words seemed to fade out as Michael began thinking about what had happened last night. He replayed what the figure had said to him in the dream, "I shall become of your world." What did that mean? Who or what was that figure? He looked up at Tom and thought about talking to him about the dream. Michael placed his coffee down.

"Hey, Tom, let me ask you something."

Tom sat up in his chair. "What's up, Mike?"

Michael started to fidget with his cup of coffee. "Well, I had this dream last night, and it was kinda strange, so I was thinking that if I told you about it, maybe you can help me try and understand it?"

"Sure. Hey, was it the one where you're naked in the quad and bikini-clad women are throwing grapes at you?"

Michael laughed. "No, man, nothing like that."

"Oh, okay. I love that dream." Tom smiled. "So let's hear it, man."

Michael proceeded to tell Tom about the dream, the place he was, and the dark figure. After he had finished, they both sat there for a brief moment in silence. Michael broke the silence first by asking, "So, what do you think, Tom?"

Tom hesitated a moment before responding. "I don't know, Mike, that's a pretty weird dream." He paused again to take a sip of his soda. "I'm sure it's nothing though. Maybe you watched some movie a while back, and it's lingering in your head. Maybe you ate something and it messed with you. Didn't Dickens say something like that once? Hell, maybe you are just nervous about going out into the real world, as they say. Shit, I know I'm nervous. I mean our last year of college, having to find and start a real job. I have to start tackling this freaking debt. I'm gonna have to find a place to live, and if I am lucky, maybe, just maybe find a sugar momma to pay for it all. It's a lot to deal with, man." Michael sat smiling, giggling slightly and nodding his head while looking at his cup of coffee. Tom continued, "Besides, people have strange dreams all the time. Hell, once I had this dream I was a camel and people kept kicking me in the nuts!"

Michael's face lit up in surprise and he began to laugh. "What? That's weird, Tom!"

Tom nodded his head as he smiled. "Yeah, tell me about it. But, hey, it just goes to show you, sometimes dreams are just dreams. They don't always have to mean something."

They both started to laugh. "I guess you're right. Thanks for listening, Tom," Michael replied.

"Hey, no problem." Tom took another sip of his soda then placed it back on the table as he continued to speak, "Hey, you know that blond girl, Lisa, in our business administration class?"

"Which one, the one that sits near that guy Bill down front?"

Tom shook his head. "No, no, the one that sits two rows ahead of us to the right."

"Oh, you mean the one that was wearing the red sweater today?"

Tom pointed at Michael. "Yeah, that's her! Oh, man, she is gorgeous! You know, I wonder if she'd wanna go out sometime."

They continued to talk about all sorts of other things as the time passed: movies, music, girls, as well as the courses they were taking at the college. Michael was beginning to feel a little better, but deep down, he was still disturbed by the dream as well as the voice he heard in it.

※

This time, Michael's dream brought him to dunes of snow and mountains of ice. He walked along a path and saw the bodies of men and women of all ages lying face down and up in the snow. Some were frozen stiff like they had been there for a long time and even some with the look of fear frozen on their face. He took notice of all this, but he didn't recall seeing any children. Some of these people seemed to have simply frozen to death, while others appear to have been slaughtered and were laying in pieces. There were spots of red snow across the ground. As he continued along, he saw something moving on some of the bodies lying near the path that he was walking on. On close inspection, he saw that spiders were laying eggs in the open wounds of many of the bodies. He felt sick when he saw the eggs hatching in one man's exposed throat. They crawled out the wound and moved down his corpse quickly as if the spiders were moving across the body like a thick fog rolling along that hugged the ground. He watched on as some of the spiders stayed on the bodies and began to eat the flesh in the open wounds. Others scattered off into the snow.

Michael continued onward. Then he noticed the trees in the distance. As he came closer, he noticed that there were yet again limbs hanging in trees and various human organs lying at the roots below. He couldn't identify them all, but he could tell what the intestines, lungs, and heart looked like. The cold kept the smell from being very strong, but even then, it wasn't enough, he could still smell the decay and rot; the iron in the blood spilled was fragrant as well. The branches of the tree were covered in blood, but it wasn't dripping down to the ground. He felt his stomach spasm at the sight of it all. His face cringed as he turned away. He hunched over and began spitting out the warm saliva that was now forming in his mouth in an effort to stop the vomit from coming. He wiped his face and caught his breath.

"Where am I?" Michael shouted as he stood up.

Then he heard the figure's voice, "You are in the place where the lost souls dwell."

This time, he could definitely tell that it was a man's voice. The figure suddenly appeared and was about ten feet from

Michael, if he had to guess. Even at that distance, he couldn't make out the figure's face. The man stood there, as once again the light did not touch upon his face, but his clothes seemed just a bit more visible this time. He could tell that he seemed to be shrouded in a garment made up of various shreds and patches of dark black and grey fabric. It covered him entirely like a cloak, which made it very difficult for Michael to make out his body structure. However, Michael could tell that the man was about six inches taller than he was, which would make him about six feet, four inches tall.

Michael responded, "Lost souls? You mean purgatory?"

"If that is what you wish to call it, Michael," the figure replied.

Michael stared in surprise. "How did you know my name?" his voice was full of inquisition and confusion.

"I know a lot about you, Michael. I have been watching you for quite some time now."

"You've been watching me? Why me?" Michael's voice cracked at the end. Now he was not only confused but frightened as well. He tried to move closer to the figure, but when he took one step, it was as if he had become frozen. He was filled with a feeling of utter dread. He was so scared he began to urinate on himself.

The dark figure replied, "I need you to help me. To help me leave this accursed place, I do not belong here. I was never meant to be here. I shall become of your world."

Michael felt the warm liquid fear running down his leg. "I-I don't understand."

"In time, I will help you understand, but for now, you must go."

Before Michael had a chance to respond, he woke up back in his bed, but this time, he wasn't sweating, and he wasn't out of breath, but he jumped out of bed suddenly with a sound of annoyance. His bed was soaked in urine.

CHAPTER 4

Monday, April 9

Michael awoke with a feeling of comfort; it had been five days since his last dream of the figure and of that horrible place. He climbed out of bed, tuned down the radio, grabbed a set of clothes, and headed in the bathroom for his normal morning routine. After a shower, he made himself some toast and a cup of coffee. The radio was still on in the background. The local college radio station was on, and he heard the radio host say, "Graduates, today is the last day for cap and gown purchases, so make sure you get yours." Michael nodded his head while hearing the announcement. Despite the as-of-late dreamless sleep, he sat there and found himself yet again pondering about the figure and why it wanted his help. He was glad he hadn't had anymore dreams, but a part of him actually wanted another dream to happen. It was that curiosity of "why me" that he wanted answered. Michael looked down at his phone. "*Shit!* Ten minutes till class, shit!" Michael gathered his things, turned off the radio, and ran out the door.

"What's up, Mike?" Tom said as Michael sat down next to him.

Michael was out of breath from running across campus to make it on time. He collapsed into his seat and looked at Tom, still trying to catch his breath. "What...did I miss?"

"Relax, Mikey, McVicker went back to get our tests. The TA is out sick and left them in his office and didn't tell him. Say, how do you think you did? Or should I even ask, you nerd!" Tom laughed as he nudged Michael's shoulder.

Prof. McVicker walked in and placed the exams down on the podium. "All right, class, let's hope that after this attempt at comprehension, you will take heed of my advice and read the chapters more than once and take better notes! People, this isn't rocket science. It's a good thing there are five of these things, but remember, you only have one left, so if you're still struggling, I suggest you make more of an effort to pull yourself up!" The professor passed out the tests and then returned to the front of the class. "Let us continue from Thursday's discussion, contractual law. As you know, there are seven types of contracts."

Tom whispered to Mike, "So, Mikey, you been havin' anymore of those weird dreams?"

"No. The last one was back on Wednesday. I think you were right though, they're just delusions created by stress. If I am being honest, I am worried about what comes after college ends."

"See, I told you so."

"Yeah, yeah, don't gimme the old Tom 'I told ya so' speech."

Tom giggled. "No sweat. Dude, dude, check out Lisa, she's wearing a skirt today. I've had it. I am gonna make a move and talk to her."

"Yeah, well, best of luck to you. I'll be ready with the ice when she turns you down."

Tom smirked and smiled at Mike. "You'll see ya prick." Tom nudged Michael.

Michael focused back on the lecture. After fifteen minutes, he found himself thinking of the figure again. He was trying to recall what his voice sounded like.

"Mr. Thompson!"

"Hunh? What?" Michael jumped as Prof. McVicker called his name.

"I said, what is the difference between a bilateral and a unilateral contract?" Prof. McVicker sounded very displeased in Michael's lack of attention.

"A bilateral is basically a promise for a promise while a unilateral is a promise for an act. A bilateral contract comes into existence when the promises are exchanged while a unilateral contract comes into existence once the act is performed."

"Correct, Mr. Thompson. Now then, who can tell me the difference between a formal and an informal contract?"

Class was over after Prof. McVicker handed back the exams. Tom sounded very excited. "All right, an eighty-nine!"

Michael sat befuddled as he stared at his paper. He had gotten a seventy-nine with a note for Michael to see Prof. McVicker after class. After all the students left, Michael told Tom that he would meet him in the cafeteria. Michael approached Prof. McVicker.

"You wanted to see me, Professor?"

"Ah, Michael! I am concerned about the performance on your last exam."

"Yeah, I… I was a little distracted this past week, but I am going to refocus, and I'm confident that I will do better on the final."

"See that you do, Michael, you have done so well up to this point, and you're a fine student. It would be a shame for you to fall below your potential."

"Yes. Thank you, Professor." Michael started to leave when the professor started again.

"Look, being that it's the end of the semester and you are graduating, what do you say if you get an A on the final, we just erase this little exam here?"

Michael was really surprised. "You would do that?"

"Why not? Your previous grades on all the other assignments coupled with your knowledge and participation are a shining example of your aptitude. I see no point in having a misstep like this affect your final grade. So, do we have a deal?"

"Yeah… I mean yes, yes, sir, we do."

"Good then, I will see you next class." Prof. McVicker extended his hand to shake Michael's. Michael responded in kind and shook his hand. "Oh, and, Mr. Thompson, do get some sleep. If I am being honest, you look awful."

"Yes, sir. Thank you, sir. Have a nice day." Michael turned and started to leave.

"You too, Michael."

Michael stopped off to use the bathroom before meeting Tom for lunch. He washed his hands and was now putting water on his face. "Hello, Michael." It was the figure's voice.

Michael spun around quickly to look behind him, but he saw nothing. He turned back around and stared at the mirror for a moment, and then he quickly scooped up some more water and splashed his face.

"I'm coming for you, Michael." The voice began to laugh.

It echoed through his ears and began to fade. Michael was about to speak when his nose started to bleed. He quickly reached for some paper towels. He turned again and looked around the bathroom once more.

"Where are you?" he demanded. "Hello? Answer me!" but he heard nothing.

Michael had already showered, gotten dressed in his sleep shorts and T-shirt, and was ready for bed, but he just paced around his room biting his fingernails. He was wondering what was going happen when he went to sleep. Where would he find himself? What would he see? After a time, he decided that it didn't make any sense to try and stay awake as he would only be delaying the inevitable. He slid into bed and closed his eyes to try and go to sleep. He tossed and turned for a while then finally settled into a position on his side with his right arm tucked under the pillows and his head. He took a few slow, deep breaths, and after a short time, he fell asleep.

He found himself in a desert. There were many dunes, the sun was shining brightly high up in the distance, and the winds blew strong. He wasn't sure why, but he felt compelled to walk forward, so he began to climb the first dune. When he reached the top, he saw what appeared to be an oasis in the distance. He took a step forward and fell down the dune. He felt the sand smacking against his face and finding its way into the different parts of his clothes as he rolled down the dune. He slid a little and then came to a stop at the bottom. He raised his head and found himself face-to-face with a man screaming for someone to save him. The man's skin appeared to have been stripped from his body. His bloody, sinewy flesh glistened in the hot sun. It reminded him of that invisible man science doll he had as a kid where one side showed all the muscles and veins but with more blood. The man was waist deep in the sands.

Michael reacted quickly and rolled way from the man onto his side. Then he stood up in horror and saw more people screaming. Some were also buried while others where just lying out along the sands. The air became filled with their sounds of agony. Michael focused in on one woman who had been disemboweled. She was trying to scoop her intestines back into her abdomen as she cried and screamed. Another person was lying on the sand and had been cut in half at the waist and was still moving. Michael thought how someone with that level of trauma could even be alive, but his mind reminded him of where he was. He looked back at the woman trying to pull herself back together and noticed that there were many vultures circling overhead, and some of them were hopping around the woman with their wings extended as they pecked at her innards and legs. The woman screamed at them to leave her alone and to go away. Michael became ill when he saw a snake emerge from the woman's genitals. He wiped the sick from his face and started moving again. Fear kicked in, and he ran across the sands. He headed up the next dune in the direction of the oasis he saw before.

"I have been waiting for you." The figure stood at the top of the dune and motioned toward Michael.

Michael paused to catch his breath, and then he asked, "Why am I here?"

"Because you need to understand what this place is before you can know who I am and why I am trapped here."

Michael turned back around and looked out at the sands. "Who are all of these people?"

"As I said before, this is the place where the lost souls dwell. The ones that are being guided, carried, or walking are the lost souls."

"Then who are all these people who are being eaten alive?"

"The ones you speak of are the damned…"

Michael was confused. "But I thought the damned went to hell?"

"Indeed, the damned do go to hell, but these are the souls of those who have taken it upon themselves to be removed from the mortal coil."

"You mean they've committed suicide?"

"Precisely."

Michael was quiet for a moment then began to speak. "Who are you?"

"You may call me Orrix."

"Orrix…" Michael was about to speak when it was as if Orrix had read his mind and replied before Michael had a chance to ask his question.

"Yes, it is time you knew where I came from as well as who I once was. So, let me quickly bring you up to speed. A long time ago, Lucifer spawned me for the purpose of turning souls."

Michael interrupted, "Wait. Lucifer? As in *the devil?*"

"Yes, exactly. I was placed in the world as a man, like you. Initially, I was to make people see that God did not care for them, that Lucifer would and could give them anything they could ever desire. If they agreed, then I would turn them. The centuries passed, and I was promoted, if you will, to a higher rank of demon. My task now was to recruit humans for Lucifer and have them ready for the apocalypse."

Michael stood in disbelief. He had been raised to believe in God and went to Sunday school, but after he was a teenager, he stopped going to church with his parents and eventually stopped believing in it all. "My god, you mean the devil is real?"

"Yes, quite."

Michael was breathing heavy, and after many attempts, he was able to gather enough strength to speak. "What do you mean your job was to turn souls?"

"Just as it means, Michael. I turned souls away from the grace of God and to the glory of Satan."

"So, how did you turn them?"

"I was given the power to drink of their blood, and once they neared death, if they wished to live, they would drink my blood, thus taking in a part of Satan and becoming his servant." Michael stood frozen with fear. It was so strong that Orrix could smell it on him. "Do not fear, Michael, I do not wish to harm you. I am merely here to help you understand."

Michael's eyes opened widely, and he struggled for the words that he knew in his heart. "You mean that you're a v-vampire?" Michael began to move backward but became frozen again. This time, he didn't know why he couldn't move. Perhaps Orrix had held him there with some kind of psychic energy, but his body wouldn't react to the urgent thoughts of him wanting to turn and run away. His eyes were locked on Orrix. He felt tears starting to well up in his eyes.

"That is what your world has come to know me and my kind as. As you may or may not know, every culture in the world has a myth or legend about my kind, but it is Lucifer who spawned me and I who spawned all those other vampires, as you humans call us."

Michael stood there motionless, he couldn't believe the things he had just heard. It seemed almost impossible to comprehend, but he thought about everything that had happened up to this point, and none if it made any sense. Michael knew that things were not always black and white, that there will always be a gray area.

Orrix began to speak again, "Now you must go."

Michael's voice was filled with a sad desperation and a longing for the truth, "Wait! Why do you keep bringing me here? Please, tell me! What the fuck do you want from me?"

"Soon, Michael, soon. I will come to you again soon, and I shall become of your world."

CHAPTER 5

Tuesday, April 10

Michael awoke on his stomach with drool coming out of his mouth. He heard something in the background. He rose up his head and with tired eyes stared at the wet spot on his pillow. Then he recognized what the sound was in the background. It was his phone, so he sat up and grabbed it. Without seeing who it was, he answered the call. His mouth was dry, and he had trouble speaking until he cleared his throat, wet his mouth and lips, then he answered, "Hello?"

"Mike, dude, where you been, man?" Tom's voice sounded concerned.

"Oh, hey, Tom. What do you mean where have I been?"

There was an urgency in Tom's response. "Mike, its twelve-thirty, you missed business law."

Michael shot up out of bed. He was fully awake now. "Oh fuck! Fuck! Goddammit!"

"Relax, Mike, I took good notes."

Michael shook his head in annoyance and quipped back at Tom, "Oh well, that makes me feel a lot better!"

"Hey, my notes aren't that bad. So, what if I write small?"

"You'd be better off writing in Braille, man. That's not the point though. I just had this conversation with McVicker how I was going to try harder, and now I miss class this close the end of the semester. I just...fuck, man."

"Look, man, just tell him you were sick. You ate something that didn't agree with you and you were laid up all day."

Michael mulled the idea over in his head. "Yeah, I guess so. I guess I need to start setting two alarms."

"Yeah, I don't know why you don't just use your phone like every other normal person," Tom said.

"Hey!" Michael snapped back. "I like waking up to the college radio station."

"Yeah, okay, whatever. Next thing I know, you'll be listening to cassette tapes. So, what were you doing last night?"

Michael sat there with his eyes closed as he rubbed his forehead.

"Mike?"

"Hunh?" Michael replied.

"I said, what were you doing last night? Were you out with someone or playing it solo at your place, if you know what I mean?" Tom laughed.

Michael laughed and responded in kind, "Ha-ha, very funny, jerk."

"Well, what were you doing? Did you have another one of those fucked up dreams you were telling me about?" Michael started to think about telling Tom about Orrix, about how he came to be, and what he was, but Michael knew that Tom wouldn't believe him, so he decided against it.

Michael began to yawn but spoke through it. "No, Tom, I just uh…stayed up late reading. Guess I dozed off around 3:00 a.m."

"Well, I already e-mailed you the notes you missed, so check 'em out and let me know if there is anything else you need, okay?

"Thanks, Tom."

"No problem, and I don't want to hear any shit about my penmanship either. Hey, don't you have a class at three?"

"Yeah, I do," Michael said as he stood up and stretched his arm up while arching his back.

"Well, roll your ass outta bed and get mobile! I'll see you later."

"All right. Thanks again, Tom."

"Hey, no problem. Later."

"See ya."

Michael ended the call and sat back down on the bed. He sat there for about five minutes before he got up to go take a shower. He stood in the shower as the water splashed down onto his face. His eyes were closed, and despite oversleeping, he felt exhausted. One question kept roaming through his mind, why had Orrix chose Michael to help him? And with that arose more questions. Like why was Orrix in purgatory in the first place? And what did he plan to do if he ever did get out? Then there was the whole vampire revelation. Michael started thinking of all the things he had read, seen, or heard about vampires. They hated crosses and churches, so being connected to Satan could square that. Then he started to remember all the ways they could be killed from the movies that he had seen and the books that he had read. Sunlight was lethal, garlic could hurt them. He remembered a scene in the movie *The Lost Boys* where they used garlic

41

and holy water to kill vampires. Then there was a stake through the heart, the aforementioned crosses could ward them away as well. Silver. *What was it about silver?* Michael wondered. Then he remembered how he had seen in some horror films that it could hurt them. Or was that werewolves? Michael decided after class that he would sit down and do some more research on vampires. If all this was true, perhaps he could learn something else that could help him.

After his classes were done for the day, Michael headed over to the college library. It was quiet, had good Wi-Fi coverage, and probably had some actual books on the subject. Michael walked up and down the aisles of the library. He was on the second floor in the fiction section. He rounded the tall oak bookshelves and stood in front of them. Looking back and forth and up and down, he found what he was looking for. He leaned forward and pulled out Bram Stoker's *Dracula* and added it to his pile. He had already grabbed some other books about mythology and the occult. He took his books and made his way to a vacant table. He plugged in his headphones, turned on some music, and started reading.

He read about the myths from other countries and the different types of vampires there were according to these books. Sometimes he thought that all this was simply ridiculous and laughed at himself for getting this far into researching all this, but something inside made him read on. He reached a part about the origins of vampires. Some believe Vlad Dracul a.k.a. Vlad Tepes, Vlad the Impaler, a.k.a. Dracula, or son of the Dracul, was the first real vampire. Most people believed this one because there was proof he lived as well as him being the most frequently used in literature and in cinema revolving around vampires. Other myths involved a woman named Elizabeth Bathory. She was tried and convicted of killing several hundred girls. She was a countess of Transylvania who had sadistic tendencies with the slaves of the castle. He read the myth of how by the time that her husband had died, she had grown old and lost her beauty. She tried to find a new lover, but her beauty was gone, so no one wanted to be with her. This rejection, coupled with the anger about how she had aged, filled her with rage that was bubbling under the surface. This rage was typically directed at her servants. One day, she struck a servant girl for an oversight and the blood that was drawn from her scratch splattered against Elizabeth's cheek. As the myth says, she could have sworn that where the blood had landed, it made her skin look younger and more pliant. This was the beginning of her massacring of the servant girls for their blood, which she bathed in to retain her beauty. Her blood lust was insatiable and many young girls were killed. Due to this myth, many people believe that she was the first vampire.

He continued looking through the books and came across the pictures of Bela Lugosi and many other stars that played the role of Dracula as well as many popular icons that played the role of vampires. The next theory he read was about how Judas was damned by God for betraying Christ and he was condemned to the night and forced to drink the blood of the living. Michael thought that it could explain the whole fixation with crosses and churches, but did that mean if Orrix was telling the truth that he was Judas? Or perhaps these books were wrong. He shook his head in disbelief at the whole scenario but continued on. He found some other instances of vampires from around the world. There were so many different cultures that had myths and names for what appeared to be vampires. They were known as *afrit* in

Arabian folklore, *aswang manananggal* from the Philippines, *giang shi* in China, *loogaroo* in the West Indies. There were many more. Clearly, vampires were something cultures all around the world encountered or at least had stories about. Michael decided to go home and see if he could find some movies or something to watch as well.

It was about eleven thirty, and Michael was watching the end of the film *Interview with a Vampire*. He fell asleep before he could see the end, and, in his dreams, he was in a city. It reminded him of San Francisco in that it was sunny and by a large bay with some bridges. The people walked on by going to work, talking with friends, and there were those driving in cars. He could hear trains traveling in the distance as well. The sun shined down on Michael. It was so bright he had to shield his eyes with his hand when he looked up. Michael breathed in the air and felt relaxed, but then Orrix appeared, and once again, the light did not shine on him, which made sense to Michael now. Orrix began to walk forward, and Michael stood frozen with his eyes locked on him.

"Hello, Michael."

Michael nervously replied, "I… I have been studying you and your kind, Orrix."

"Yes, I know. So, tell me did you like the movie?"

Michael was startled. How could he know that he was watching a movie?

"How do I know, Michael? I have been watching you, remember? We are always watching. I may not be in hell anymore, but there are demons who find things out for me, and they find ways of getting the information back to me."

Michael stood there wanting to speak, but he couldn't find the words.

"Perhaps now I shall explain to you the nature of my kind. All those books you people have written, all those movies you have are nothing but lies. Lies conceived and dispersed by yours truly. You see, I have taken great efforts throughout time to convince the world that my kind does not exist. To make you humans believe that we are merely a myth, a story, nothing more. Vlad Dracul for example, he was merely a scapegoat. I had heard that Bram Stoker was writing a book about Vlad Dracula. He had decided to use the local legends about him to write a story. It was partially my fault having vampires roaming around during Vlad's battles with the Turks. You see, my spawns were like vultures on the battlefield, and bodies would be found drained of blood. Naturally, they figured Vlad did it because he was so brutal and ruthless. Vlad didn't deny it because it bolstered his cause. Well, Bram was looking for historians to help make his writing more accurate, so I posed as a historian. So, I simply used the myths that were already circulating and twisted them to ensure it focused wholly on Vlad.

"Bram was grateful for my efforts, and it seemed to work, which helped to take attention away from me personally. I have done this a few times actually. I would spend time in taverns throughout the years or have my spawn do it for me to spread legends and lies. For instance, Mr. J. Sheridan Le Fanu, his novel *Carmilla*, helped relieve attention from my kind and myself as well for a time. I needed to do this because in the year 1047, the Russians came to be aware of my kind when they suspected a prince I had turned was more than just a man. They called him *Upir Lichy*, meaning wicked vampire. It was around that time that I decided it was time to begin concealing my kind and myself much more than before. With all these myths and stories, it was just a matter of time before many of your famous writers began to write of my kind. Writers like Poe, Hoffman, and Goethe, to name a few. Did you know that some time ago, they exhumed the graves of Vlad Dracul and Bram Stoker? Do you know what they found, Michael?"

Michael stared with his eyes fixed on Orrix. He dared not remove them. "No. What did they find?"

"Nothing. I removed their bodies to avoid them doing further research and only to learn that the stories about Vlad being the real source or my kind was not true. Plus, my doing so just added to the myth. It was a fair amount of effort keeping your kind from learning the truth. Now as for all these falsehoods you humans have concocted about how to harm us and what we can and cannot do. One thing your kind has been able to get right over the centuries was sunlight. As you see me now, the sun shines, but light does not touch me. God has always been referred to as the light, and because of that, my spawn cannot be in the sunlight."

Michael was almost scared to ask but doing so made him feel a little at ease knowing that Orrix was not invincible, so he interjected. "Does that mean if you stay out in the light you will die?"

"Wrong, Michael. You didn't allow me to finish. My spawn cannot be in the sunlight. For myself, well I am the first and oldest demon spawned by Lucifer. Because of this, I was afforded great satanic powers, and thus the light cannot harm me. As for this," Orrix motioned to his face cloaked in shadow, "it is part of my curse for being trapped here. I never knew how dreadful it could be to never be able to feel the sun again. So, here I stand, punished in the light of the sun, denied its warmth. As for my spawn, it would seem that while I was given all the power a demon could ask for, I couldn't protect my own spawn from the light."

Michael could sense the anger and frustration in his voice. He was also very curious as to how Orrix ended up in this place. He began to speak, but Orrix cut him off. His anger was palpable now.

"I shall see you again soon. Then we will discuss why I am here."

Orrix began to walk away when Michael stepped toward him and started, "Hey, wait a minute." There was a slight irritation in his voice. "I have more questions that I wan—"

"Silence!" Orrix was suddenly in front of Michael and holding him by the throat. Michael was elevated nearly a foot off the ground, and he felt a tightness in his chest as well as his throat. "You shall demand nothing of me! When the time is right, you will know all that I have to tell. Do not take such tones with me, mortal. This time I shall let you live, but if you try such insolence with me again, I will not hesitate to tear you limb from limb and bathe in your blood! Now go!"

Michael fell to the ground as Orrix seemed to disappear into nothingness. He lay in a fetal position clenching his chest. It was then that he heard the screeching of tires followed by the sounds of a car crashing into something. He looked up, and he saw that the buildings of the city were on fire, and the bodies of men and women were falling from now shattered windows covered in flames were falling from now shattered windows. A large earthquake started, and Michael saw large cracks in the ground open up. Large, hulking demons began pouring out of the cracks. People were running in panic as the demons ran up and down the streets grabbing people and throwing them over their shoulders as cries of terror and screams for mercy echoed loudly through his ears. He watched as these demons started returning to the cracks and throwing the people down into the now open ground then turning around and running back for more. All around him was pain and suffering, and he felt trapped and needed to break free. He rose to his feet to run, but when he turned to go, there was a woman in front of him with maggots protruding from her mouth. He shoved her aside and began to run. He ran about twenty feet when he tripped and fell, his face smacking against the pavement.

Michael awoke and shot up in his bed. His breathing was erratic and heavy, and his sweat soaked clothes weighed down upon him making him feel very uncomfortable. Then for some reason that he could not understand, he began to cry.

CHAPTER 6

Saturday, April 14

Michael hadn't slept more than ten minutes at a time in four days. It was midafternoon on Saturday, and he was in the local pharmacy buying NoDoz and caffeine pills to help him stay awake. He leaned against the shelf and shut his eyes for a second then opened them just as quickly. Michael feared what might happen if he returned to that awful place and saw Orrix there. Up to this point, Michael had no clue that he could be affected in his dreams. He had seen some terrible things, and despite the massive fear he felt, he never once came into harm's way despite the horrors around him. Michael now knew that Orrix was powerful and that he stood no chance against him in purgatory if he ever did try to retaliate. He figured that the best thing to do would be to avoid Orrix, but he knew he couldn't do that forever. Michael walked up to the register as the cashier was staring at him with inquisitive eyes. Michael knew that his eyes had to look swollen and that he looked utterly exhausted. Michael ignored the stares and paid for his merchandise then returned back to his apartment.

It was about three in the afternoon when the phone rang. It was Tom.

"Hey, Mike! What's happening?"

Michael was excited that it was Tom. The phone call gave him a much-needed distraction. "Hey, Tom! What's up? How you doing?"

"I'm all right, thanks. What are you doing?"

"Oh, not much, I just went and picked up some vitamins."

"Cool. Hey, I met these two girls at lunch, and I asked them to come down to Black Jack's tonight. So, you're going."

"Oh, am I?" Michael asked in playfully inquisitive manner.

"Yeah, dude, these girls are cool and super good-looking! You gotta come! I was telling one of them all about you today at lunch. So, meet me there at ten, and don't be a flake! If you skip out on this, I'll haunt your dreams." Tom laughed but heard nothing from Michael on the other end. That was when he realized what he had said. "Oh, hey, listen, man, I'm sorry. That was a stupid thing to say." Michael was biting his lower lip, trying not to snap at Tom. "Listen, Mike, I'm really sorry about that, but let me make it up to you. I am certain you could use the distraction and a night out to feel a bit of normal, college life is just the ticket. You better listen to me, man, after all, I'm in pre-med."

Michael giggled. "You're an economics major, you schmuck." Michael could sense Tom's smile through the phone.

"Ah well, you know what I mean, man. Look, I promise this will be a good time. So, please, just meet us at Black Jack's tonight, okay?"

Michael hesitated slightly but decided it was a good idea. "Um…okay. I'll see you later."

"Awesome. Awesome. I'll see you later, man."

"Okay. Later, Tom." Michael ended the call and sat down on the couch. "Well I guess it is time I went out and did something for a change and take my mind off of this situation," he said.

Prior to getting ready for the night, Michael had just finished playing a video game, which was also helping him stay awake and take his mind of things. He was playing electronic music on his phone while he stood in the bathroom shaving. He put on some aftershave balm then put on an orange, blue, and gray checkered short sleeve button-down shirt with dark-blue jeans. He sat on the end of the bed putting on his black, zip-up boots. He stood up and made sure his pant legs covered the uppers of his boots. He sprayed on some cologne then went into the bathroom to grab a couple of NoDoz pills, then he was out the door.

"ID?" The bouncer stood there defiantly with his hand extended and open waiting for Michael's ID. The muffled music from inside pulsated, threatening to burst through the buildings structure with each bass hit.

Michael reached into his back pocket to remove his wallet and then his ID. "No problem," he replied.

"Thank you... Michael," the bouncer replied. "Show your ID to the camera and have a good time."

Michael flashed his ID at the camera and held it there for a second after which he walked over to the register. The cashier looked up from his phone and addressed Michael, "That'll be five dollars."

Michael paid the cashier and walked toward the bar. There were lots of people, and the music was loud. The bass of the music sent vibrations up his body. He looked over at the dance floor and saw people dancing. The air was aglow with stage lights, especially as they bounced of the disco ball hanging above the dance floor. He began to pan the room looking for Tom. Then somebody tapped him on the shoulder.

"Hey, Mikey!"

Michael turned. "What's up, Tom!"

"Mike, this girl is dying to meet you, man! Get yourself a drink and get over here!"

"All right, all right I'll be right there!" Michael walked up to the bar and made his way through a group of four then stood at opening at the bar waiting for the bartender to notice him. She did and came over.

"What can I get ya?" she said.

Michael had a hard time hearing her, but he knew what she said. "Can I get a Jameson and ginger, please!"

The bartender nodded and walked away to make the drink. She returned and placed it down in front Michael on a napkin. "That'll be six dollars." He noticed how attractive the bartender was. Her hair was a strawberry blond, and her eyes were green. She was thin but had a muscular tone in her arms. Michael also felt a little embarrassed when he found himself noticing that her breasts were fairly exposed and pushed up high in her shirt. He caught himself and quickly looked away. He hoped that she didn't see him looking. He handed her a ten-dollar bill and told her to keep the change. Michael made his way through the crowd trying not to spill his drink. Tom and the two girls had a table about ten feet from the dance floor.

Tom stood up as Michael approached. "Mike!" He motioned to the two girls sitting down. "Mike, allow me to introduce Olivia and Kayla."

Michael greeted them and sat down next to Olivia. Tom had already had his arm around Kayla. She was attractive, her hair was up, and on looks alone, she was the typical girl Tom went for: blond hair, blue eyes, big breasts. Michael looked at Olivia and leaned in to start a conversation. He had to almost yell in order for her to hear him.

"So, are you a student here?" Michael asked.

Olivia leaned in to listen. "Yeah, this is my second year."

"So, what's your major?"

"Psychology. How about you?"

"I'm an MIS major." Michael noticed that she looked confused. "You know, Management Information Systems. It's a computer business degree."

Olivia's eyes lit up in recognition. "Oh yeah! Okay, my friend Danny is in that. So, how do you like the courses?"

"They are good, but some of them can be hellish sometimes. I have to take some programming courses, and they can get tough."

"Yeah, I know what you mean." Olivia giggled. "Well, not the programming, but I know what you mean about hellish courses."

Even though Michael was deeply engaged in conversation, he kept noticing how attractive she was. He noticed her various features in turn. She had light-brown hair and beautiful hazel eyes with just a bit greener than brown. She had an average build, and if Michael had to guess, she's about five foot five or six inches tall. Michael thought that she had a beautiful face, especially her smile. Michael felt much better now that he was out and doing something. Not even his fatigue seemed to bother him anymore.

After their conversation, Olivia and Kayla went to the bathroom while Tom and Michael waited at the table.

"So, what do you think, Mikey? Do I know how to pick 'em, or do I know how to pick 'em?" Tom sat back in his chair, smiling and waiting for affirmation.

"Yeah, Olivia seems very nice, pretty too." Michael looked over toward the bathrooms where the girls had gone.

"Yeah, Kayla is slammin'. If I play my cards right, Mikey, I could be making breakfast for two!"

Michael quipped, "Well, I do like French toast, but don't burn it this time."

Tom shoved Michael on the shoulder while laughing. "Hey, screw you, man! I may come off a little forward, but I'm a nice and respectful guy. If she's not into it, that's okay, but if that happens, well, you better bring the syrup." They both started laughing. The two girls returned.

Kayla motioned toward Tom. "C'mon Tom, I wanna dance."

Tom hopped out of the table. "You got it! Let's go! Come on you two! Woo!"

Then Olivia looked at Michael. "So…" Olivia brushed her hair back. "Do you wanna dance, Mike?"

"Yeah, sure." Michael put down his drink and made his way toward the dance floor. She held his hand and led him forward, but as they were walking, Michael thought he saw a man across the room in a cloak, like the one in his dreams. He froze.

"Orrix!" Michael surprised himself that he had shouted.

Olivia turned inquisitively. "What was that, Mike?"

Michael caught himself. "Hunh? Oh, nothing, Olivia. Come on, let's go." Michael eyes began to look around for the figure he saw. Then through a group, he saw the figure walk into the bathroom. "Hey, Olivia, I'll be right back, I'm sorry, but I have to use the restroom. I'll be right back."

Olivia was caught off guard and stood there dumbfounded. "Oh…well…okay. I'll wait here." Olivia started to dance by herself as Michael hurried across the room toward the bathroom. He entered the bathroom, and there were a few people in the restroom. He stood near the entrance breathing heavily. Wide eyed, he started looking around for Orrix. After several moments and a couple awkward stares from two of the guys in the restroom, he didn't see him. He went over to one of the sinks and splashed some water on his face. Just as he was about to leave, he saw the cloak under one of the stalls. He moved slowly toward it and braced himself.

He took a deep breath, stood in front of the door ready to act, and then he kicked open the door. "Orrix!" he shouted. It was a man in a black overcoat pulling up his pants from using the toilet. The man was shocked.

"Jesus Christ! What the hell is your problem, man?" The man was quickly putting his pants back on.

Michael relaxed as he realized he was mistaken and felt really embarrassed "Oh shit. I'm sorry, man." He quickly came up with a story. "I thought you were a friend of mine, and I was just trying to mess with him. I'm so sorry." Michael raised his hands in an apologetic fashion and quickly exited the restroom. He made his way back out to the dance floor with great speed. Olivia noticed some of the water on his brow.

"Mike, is everything all right?" Olivia asked.

"Yeah…everything is fine. C'mon, let's dance." Michael pulled her in close and started dancing to the electronic music.

At about three in the morning, Olivia and Mike ended up at his place. They were sitting on the couch, and he was talking to her about his classes, about Tom, and how long they've been friends. Olivia responded by talking about her major, psychology. She was saying how certain areas interested her and that was what made her want to study it. Then Olivia brought up the topic of dreams and that was, as she said, "Right up there as one of the things that interested me the most. They say dreams can tell you a lot about what's going on with someone."

Michael considered telling Olivia about the dreams that he had been having, but he worried that she would get weirded out and leave. After all, they had just met.

Olivia moved in closer. "You have beautiful green eyes, Michael."

Michael smiled. "I like yours too."

"Did you know in some countries green eyes are a sign of power?"

Michael felt himself blush and smile. "Really?"

"Sure." Michael noticed that Olivia was getting closer still. Then she continued, "Look at China. Jade is green and has great meaning over there."

"You have really nice skin." Michael traced his fingers across her cheek, down her neck and to her shoulder. They looked into each other's eyes and began to kiss. It was then that Michael heard a sound in the bathroom. He pulled away. "Did you hear that?"

"Hear what?" Olivia began to kiss him again. Her hand traveled over his chest and down to his side. He heard the sound again.

Michael pushed her away. "Wait, stop."

"What is it, Mike? Don't you find me attractive?" Olivia asked expectantly.

Michael turned to the bathroom. "You didn't just hear that sound?"

"Mike, I don't know what you are talking about. Are you all right?"

Michael took a breath. "I think you should go."

Olivia sat straight up. "What!" She was simultaneously surprised and insulted.

Michael stood up and created some space between himself and Olivia. "I mean it. Look, I had a great time and perhaps we can do it again, but I'm sorry, I really think you should go home. I have been going through some stuff lately, and I just need to be alone. I'm really sorry."

Olivia stood up and was visibly very frustrated. "I can't believe this. You know what, fine. If that's what you want." She made her way toward the door when Michael took a few steps toward her and called her.

"Olivia. C'mon, don't be like that." Olivia stopped and turned toward him as Michael continued, "Look, I just don't want this to be just a one-night fling, that's all. I think you are easy to talk to, I had a lot of fun tonight. You're very attractive, and I would be crazy to turn you down, but I have to be honest when I say I haven't been sleeping well lately, I've been under a lot of stress, and I just don't want either of use to regret this."

Olivia moved away from the door back toward Michael slightly.

"Mike, I had a nice time too, and I know I can be a little forward, but what can I say? I like you too. I had a nice time, and

I just wanted to keep that going, but I get it. I just felt a little insulted and rejected is all."

Michael felt his shoulders relax a bit. "I'm sorry, I didn't mean to make you feel that way, truly. So, in the vain of sounding somewhat cliché, can I have your number so I can text you or call you sometime soon so we can try this again?"

Olivia moved close to Michael. She placed her hand on his cheek and moved it around to the back of his neck. "I'm sorry you're not sleeping well, but we could be sleeping well together."

Michael's eyes closed as he let out a breath. "Oh, man. You weren't kidding. You are forward, but I am sure."

Olivia hesitated for a moment. "You want to give me your phone?" Michael unlocked his phone and handed it to Olivia. She opened the messages app and sent herself a text then handed the phone back to Michael. Michael looked at the phone and saw two emojis. A kissing face followed by a frown face. She placed her hand on his chest as if feeling his heartbeat. "Are you sure you don't want me to stay?"

He had a look of hesitation in his expression. "Um…yeah, I think so. I mean, yes, yes, I am sure."

Olivia grinned slightly. "Okay, Mike. I hope I hear from you soon. See ya." She turned and began to walk away.

Michael caught himself, "Oh, hey, can I call you a car or something?"

Olivia turned back, "No that's okay. I got it covered. Night Mike." She smiled and started away again.

"Night, Olivia." Michael shut the door. He leaned up against it and let out a big sigh. His simultaneous enjoyment and regret of the moment were shattered when he heard the noise again. He straightened up then made his way toward the bathroom slowly and quietly. He stood outside the doorway, preparing to peek his head in and find something. He wasn't sure what he would find, but there was a great suspense in him, and it felt terrible. His head inched in and saw nothing. The shower door was open, and it was empty. He let out a big breath and placed his hands on the sink. It was then that he noticed that the caffeine pills were gone. The empty bottles lay in the sink. His mouth dropped open as if he had just lost all control of his jaw. He looked around the sink and on the floor. He opened the medicine cabinet and began to shuffle through everything looking for his pills but found nothing.

He walked out of the bathroom and toward the kitchen to make some coffee. His heart began to race as he began to feel tired. All the dancing and staying out late was finally catching up to him. He didn't know if he could make it through another day without a proper sleep. He remembered hearing once that people who don't sleep for great lengths of time begin to hallucinate and can even go insane and, even worse, die. He put the coffee pot that his father had given him in the sink, filled it with water, put some coffee in the basket, covered it, and then placed it on the stove. He sat down at the table and waited. He cursed himself for not getting an electric pot, or even a capsule unit, but his father always insisted that percolator coffee was the best. His eyes were getting tired and heavy. He began to yawn then shut his eyes for a moment. He opened them quickly as if waking up to an ear-deafening sound. He dared not go to sleep. He stood up and started to pace in the kitchen while he waited. When the percolator finished, he poured himself a cup and added nothing to the dark, anti-sleep elixir. He took his cup of coffee, sat on the couch, and turned on the television. None of the channels seemed to be working, so he stood up and went to turn on the stereo. The local college station was playing some hard rock and turned the volume up as loud as he thought he could get away with at this late hour. He returned to the couch and sat down, but he did not lean back. He sat forward with his elbows on his knees. His right leg was shaking as he bounced his heel up and down. He began to yawn as he leaned back into the couch. Thirty minutes later, he was asleep.

Michael found himself in a jungle clearing. He saw people walking around like lost children. Mouths agape, looking around as if hoping to find someone who could help them. They walked a bit then stopped randomly while looking around with utter confusion and despair then after a few moments continued onward. He noticed some of them had slit wrists and marks around their necks. Michael figured that they all must have been people who committed suicide. Others had very pale skin and their lips were blue. Michael figured that was either from the hanging or drowning, but one of these people bumped into Michael, and he noticed what looked like swollen, infected, puss ridden, injection holes in the crook of their elbow. The person moved along, not fazed by the encounter.

Then Michael noticed a body lying on a rock. He could tell that it was a man. His back faced up toward Michael. Michael walked toward the man and heard noises of agony and pain that seemed to be coming from the man. Despite the fear rising in him, Michael continued to move closer and extended his hand hesitantly to see if the man was okay. As soon as Michael touched the man, the man shot up off the rock with his back still to Michael. The man extended his arms up into the air and began to scream. It was then that the man burst into flames. His body began to burn as he turned to face Michael. The flesh and muscle from his emaciated face began to both disintegrate and melt as it exposed his skull underneath. The smell of burnt hair and flesh made Michael feel very sick. Michael stood in horror and watched as blood began to pour from the man's orifices. Then as the man collapsed, a huge wave of fire shot from the man's body. It shot out in a circle and burned everything in its path instantaneously. Michael instinctively crouched down in fear and covered his head then started to scream as well. The fire did pass over Michael, but he was unaffected.

Michael stood up, checked himself, and after realizing he was okay, he turned to look at the remnants of the jungle. Those he saw walking aimlessly before now lay on the jungle floor, smoldering and smoking. The smell was awful, and Michael began to walk toward a tall tree that was now burned. He leaned against the tree and vomited. As he rose, he noticed that the branches of the tree stood leafless as burnt flesh dripped down off them to the ground below at his feet. When Michael looked back up to the top, he saw Orrix. He descended from the treetop, coming down quickly then striking down on the ground below merely feet from Michael. Michael stood there filled with both fear and wonderment.

Michael took a breath then spoke. "Why have you brought me here, Orrix?"

"Michael, Michael. Don't you remember? It is time that you know why I am stuck here in this wonderful place." Orrix said sarcastically as he motioned to his left. "Walk with me, Michael." They began to walk down a path, and Orrix began to speak once again. "As I told you before, I was spawned by Lucifer to help turn the souls of humans as an act of revenge and spite against God. I had been doing this for almost three thousand years, and you'd be amazed at how hard it was to stay around that long. Sometimes, I would have to go back to hell or simply hide for decades at a time to allow enough time to pass. Entire lifetimes spent hiding my true nature so civilization wouldn't outright discover me. Hence all the stories, legends, and myths. Lucifer always said it was better to act slowly from within and let the decay grow. He would always say that it is sometimes best to lay and wait like a snake and wait for the moment to come to you." The two stopped near a downed tree. Orrix motioned for Michael to sit down, so he did. Then Orrix continued.

"Now, around the beginning of the nineteenth century, I began to create quite a following in the depths of hell. Other demons respected my tireless efforts and admired my powers, even if limited in comparison to Lucifer's. They started swearing their allegiance to me, and this created a slow, but steady uproar in hell. Apparently, the demons saw a power in me that they believed would be able to remove Lucifer from his throne. As you may or may not know, Lucifer is an angel who was created by God, and in time, Lucifer chose to fight God for his throne. Many angels sided with Lucifer and chose to take on God, thinking they could indeed succeed." Orrix paused for a moment. "You know the outcome of that war, I'm sure. Well, in this case, we have a similar problem. Demons from all levels of hell confronted me with the proposition to rebel against Satan and take over hell. I was adamant and told them that I wanted nothing to do with it, but they continued to conspire. Despite my reassurance to Lucifer that I was not involved and his strict and brutal methods of quelling other demons who spoke of such things, whispers continued, like the ever-burning embers of the seventh circle." Orrix motioned for Michael to follow him once more. "Come, let's walk some more." They came to a hilltop that overlooked the jungle. Michael was fixated on Orrix. He was listening eagerly. Then Orrix continued.

"Around the year 1885, Lucifer was growing tired of the rebellion in hell and decided to punish all those who defied him in the worst way with the goal of setting an example. Keep in mind he had been punishing demons for disloyalty and disobedience for centuries, but this time, he held everyone who held a shred of doubt accountable. Hell had turned into a slaughterhouse for demons. He began to round up demons by the hundreds. When he caught them, there was no torture. There was no interrogation or persuasion to admit guilt, he simply destroyed them. As for me, a few demons, being the lying untrusted worthy sort that they are, decided to tell Lucifer that I was the one behind the rebellion. Despite my protestations over the years, Lucifer had enough. He wasn't about to let even a chance that this could be true go on. So, he decided to destroy all those that were left of my kind. Thousands of my own slaughtered by the lying words of a couple of demons. Centuries of effort on my part undone in a matter of moments. And so many countless others destroyed because of this lie. When I asked why, he simply told me it was a cleansing and that this is how things work to maintain order. Shortly after the eradication of the last of my kind, Lucifer brought me before him. Despite my arguments and as much as I swore my allegiance, Lucifer decided to banish me in this place of suffering for all eternity. Now I must break free of this place and return to where I belong."

Michael interrupted, "You mean hell?"

ਮੈਨੂੰ

Orrix paused for a moment. "Michael, I must return to my rightful place, and you are going to help me get there."

Michael hesitated. "And if I refuse?"

Orrix laughed. "You can't, Michael. Understand that I have eternity in this place, and if you thought me elevating you and squeezing your heart tight was pain and suffering, then you will come to know the true meaning of the word pain. You will suffer like no man has ever suffered. I will torture you night after night until you realize that you really have no choice."

"But why me? Why me! Why not someone else?"

"I am glad you asked, Michael. There is a great force in you, Michael, a force I have not seen in hundreds of years. You see, long ago in the year 1494, there was book written by Heinrich Matheson and Jacob Baker. Heinrich was a priest and Jacob was a soldier. The book was called *The Volumenus Nox Noctis*, the book of darkness. All the information contained within was recited by both the Archangel Gabriel and the angel of death. The angels told them that knowledge contained inside was gathered after the war in heaven. It contains hundreds of pages about Lucifer and his kind as well as the powers of evil. In this book, there is a section that describes ways on how to free the souls of those wrongly trapped in purgatory. You see, anyone sent here by anyone other than God can be set free by the power of God. Gabriel forbid the two from making copies of the book as they feared it would fall into the wrong hands. Armed with this knowledge, Heinrich and Jacob had started a group of holy crusaders sworn to rid the world of evil.

"After many years and some great victories, even over some of my own kind, heaven took note of their success and saw their numbers growing. So, Gabriel returned and bestowed six more copies of the book onto them. Over the centuries, their group hunted down demons and evil throughout the world in hopes of vanquishing it. During the eighteenth century, the descendants of Jacob decided that after many centuries of trying to protect seven copies of this book, it was too dangerous to have seven copies circulating around the world and that it would be just a matter of time before evil would obtain one if not all them. Since Gabriel had forbid more copies being made, they knew if this knowledge was lost, their cause would be doomed. Jacob's descendent, Aeron, convinced the others to have six copies destroyed, and Heinrich's descendant, Tarah, was entrusted with the original. In 1803 Tarah sent the book to America. It was kept in a monastery and was circulated over the years to keep evil from finding it, but now I know where it is."

Michael was engrossed in the story now. "How did you find it?" Michael asked eagerly.

"The year was 1885, and I had been searching for the book in hopes of destroying the last copy so that all the knowledge that was given to man about Lucifer, hell, and purgatory would be destroyed and lost. But as I told you before, I was damned to this place by him." There was an irritation in his voice now. "But before I was sent to this place, I found the location of the book, and it is my belief that it is still there today."

Michael looked at Orrix inquisitively. "So, how do I fit into all of this?"

"In 1775, my kind and I hunted down the last of Heinrich's and Jacob's clan of hunters and slaughtered them and their families to eliminate the chance of an ancestor coming to rise up against us. Many of my kind were destroyed doing so, and only a few dozen of my kind remained. However, apparently, one of

Heinrich's descendants had an affair with a girl here in America. She had a son, which became your ancestor. Which brings us to you."

Michael shook his head in disbelief. "Wait a minute! Okay, so what you're saying is that I am a descendant of this guy Heinrich? That's crazy!"

"How is that crazy, Michael? You humans are promiscuous by nature. Your whole species lives to procreate and spread like a disease. The fact of the matter is your bloodline leads back to Heinrich, and in you is a great, albeit dormant power. It is that power which will lead you to the book for me."

Michael stood there silent and in disbelief. "I… I just can't believe—"

"Believe it, Michael. The sooner you accept this, the sooner you can begin to move on. Don't bother resisting me, Michael. You are fully aware of the consequences if you disobey."

Michael stood there silent, mulling over his options but struggled to find any. He was quiet for what felt like minutes when he finally sighed. "I guess I really do have no choice." Michael hung his head and began to breathe slowly. He closed his mouth and began to bite his bottom lip. "So, if I help you get this book, you'll leave me alone?"

"Precisely, Michael."

Michael sighed again. "All right." He looked up at Orrix. "Where is this book?"

"Very good. I have been able to use what power I have to reach out, and I feel that the book is in this area, in an old house off route 34. I can sense it, but I am not certain of its exact location as my powers are blunted by this place."

Michael quizzically looked at Orrix. "But route 34 isn't exactly small. It could be anywhere. How am I—" Michael's chest started to hurt again."

Orrix faced Michael. "Don't interrupt me again. I am working on finding it and will contact you soon. Until then, sleep well."

Michael awoke on the couch. The radio was still on but playing some easy listening music now. Michael looked over at the clock radio and saw it was about seven in the morning. He lay back into the couch and felt his body sink into the cushions. Michael needed help. He knew in his heart he couldn't do this alone. Michael decided that he was going to tell Tom everything and hoped he would help. He just couldn't figure out how to tell him this. Up to this point, he had told Tom some pretty crazy stuff, and despite Tom's sporadic quips and sarcasm, he had been pretty understanding, but this was next-level stuff. If Tom didn't believe him, what would he do?

CHAPTER 7

Sunday, April 22

Michael had woken up several times during the night. On and off for the past seven days, when he did dream, they were nothing but nightmares, but not the same as the ones with Orrix. These seemed like your average nightmares where he would be falling or running from someone and then wake up with a jolt or sense of dread, but he couldn't help but think how they dulled in comparison to the images of that place. Regardless, they made him uneasy and caused him more restlessness. Michael had thought that he had seen images of Orrix in his dreams, but there was no real contact like in the other dreams, so he couldn't be certain. Eventually Michael, did have some dreamless sleep and with that had slept in till about two in the afternoon.

When he woke up, he decided to call Olivia and see if she wanted to go to the movies. He had gone on a few small lunch dates with her since their first night together. The first of which was awkward for just a little bit, but Olivia said she understood what had happened, and they both agreed to move past it and try again. So, Michael was taking it slow. He was intrigued by her and wanted to get to know her more before complicating things with sex. Tom kept ragging on him how he couldn't believe that he hadn't sleep with her already, but Michael was starting to really like her and wanted things to be right. Michael thought about just texting her, but he had always preferred to speak to people on the phone. He found her number, tapped it in to his phone, and the line started to ring.

Olivia answered on the third ring. "Hello?"

Michael replied, "Hey, Olivia?"

"Mike!" There was excitement in her voice. "How's it going? Did you just wake up?"

"Yeah. I figured I would give you a call and see what you are up to tonight."

"You woke up and decided to call me? That's really sweet, Mike." Michael could hear her smiling.

"I know this is kinda short notice, but would you want to come to the movies with me tonight?"

"Well, I had some plans, but it's nothing I can't break."

Michael smiled. "Great, can I come by around six thirty tonight? The movie is at seven fifteen."

"Sure, that would be nice."

Again, Michael smiled. "Great, then I will see you then."

"Okay. See ya."

"All right, great." Michael caught himself "Oh wait! You know I just realized, I don't know where you live."

Olivia giggled. "How about I just meet you at your place?"

"Sure, that would be fine. You remember how to get here?"

"Yeah, I got a good look at the area when you rushed me out of your apartment last weekend, remember?" There was a playful sarcasm in her voice.

Michael smiled. "Okay, okay. Well, consider this me formally making up for that night. The lunches and coffee meetups from this past week don't count. So, I'll see you at six thirty tonight?"

"See you then, Mike."

"Okay, bye." He hung up the phone and stood there with a smile on his face then made his way to the bathroom.

At 6:32 p.m., Michael heard a knock at the door.

Michael yelled from inside, "It's open, Olivia! C'mon in!" Michael was in the bedroom putting on his shirt. He made his way out into the living room. Michael stopped and stared at her. "Wow, you look great!"

She was in a red flowery dress that went down just above her knees. Her hair was up, and from what he could see, she had little makeup. She had a very natural look to her, and she was pretty, which Michael liked. He couldn't help but notice how the dress accented her curves in all the right ways.

"Are you ready to go Mike?"

"Yeah. Like I said, I figured we would go over to the movies first. There is this new comedy out, *Wedding Party*, about how this wedding just goes completely wrong."

Olivia cut him off, "Oh the one with Tim Roberts? He is so funny, but you know what movie I would like to see, the new horror movie, *The Pain Within*. I have always been drawn to those kinds of movies."

There was a slight hesitation in his voice. "Oh, okay." The word *horror* couldn't but help make him think of Orrix. "What time is the next showing?"

"It's at eight fifteen, but we don't have to go if you don't want to."

Michael smiled. "No, it's okay."

"Are you sure? You didn't order the tickets already, did you?" Olivia asked.

Michael waved his hand at the comment as to wave it off, "No, no. Well I did, but I can get a refund on them. We have time still." Michael unlocked his phone and proceeded to request a refund from the movie ticket app. "Done. Gotta love technology." The two laughed.

Olivia leaned in and grabbed Michael by the arm. "Besides, now we have time to grab a bite to eat beforehand."

"That's a great idea." They started to walk out of Michael's apartment, and Michael shut the door when he continued, "I won't eat too much though because I plan on getting a big bucket of buttered popcorn. Plus, I want to make sure we have enough time to eat and not be late for the film. I don't want to miss the coming attractions. They are my favorite part."

"I love the coming attractions too!" Olivia smiled. "We can whisper about which ones we would or would not want to see."

Michael smiled again, and they headed out of the building toward the theater to find a place to eat. They ended up grabbing some pizza and talked about the upcoming finals and then changed the topic to their favorite movies. Michael was pleased to see that despite the horror films, they had a lot in common in that regard. Michael didn't dislike horror films, but they just weren't his go-to genre. He was more into science fiction and action films. They finished their food, paid, then left the pizzeria to head to the movies. They arrived at the theater with fifteen minutes until the movie started. Michael pulled out his wallet.

"It's on me."

Olivia rebutted, "But you already paid for dinner. You have to let me contribute a little. It's only fair after all."

"Please? I insist, it's the least I can do after how I acted last time. I was being a little weird."

"All right, but as long as you let me pay for popcorn and stuff?" Olivia insisted.

"Deal." Michael looked up toward the ticket man. "Two for *The Pain Within*, please."

After the movie, they made their way out of the theater and headed back toward Michael's apartment. They were quiet for the first few minutes of the walk. There was the occasional stare and smile. Then Michael began the conversation.

"So, what did you think of the movie?"

"Well, I would have to say it was more suspense than horror, but I guess that I can see why people are calling it a horror film. It didn't happen much, but when it did, there was so much gore in it. So that was kinda gross, and I could see how it could border on a slasher-film-type movie."

Michael reached over and grabbed Olivia's hand. They both smiled. "Yeah. I think the reveal at the end was kinda bad."

Olivia looked at Michael inquisitively "What do you mean? It was so true to life."

Michael smirked. "Oh yeah? How so?"

"Well, look at the premise of the movie. It's about a man who kills because he likes to kill. Yes, throughout the movie, you are thinking about why he is doing what he is doing, but when it came to the end, you're told he kills these people simply because he likes it. I mean that's how this world is sometimes, right?"

Michael thought about it. "Yeah, I guess you're right when you put it that way. I just kind of wish they ended the film. So many horror films have to leave us with this moment where we think it's simply going to end and the people go on and live their lives, but then they do the last-minute scare where the killer lives or has gotten away and bum bah bum, sequel time!"

Olivia laughed. "Yeah, that's true. Even in this film, look at the very end of the movie. The main star dies and the killer gets away. So, I see what you're saying, but I kind saw it as being true to life because there are so many unsolved crimes in this world. And not to be a downer or anything, but that's what life is most times, depressing."

"Well, I guess that's one way to look at it." He knew she had a point. Life can be a series of dejected moments. They continued to walk and talk, then five minutes later, they were back at Michael's. Once they got back into Michael's apartment, they sat down on the couch and continued their conversation. Michael had poured some iced tea that he made yesterday.

Olivia was still talking about movies. "I dunno what it is, Michael, but I have always liked those kinds of movies. A lot of people think that it's weird for someone like me to like this kinda stuff. You know a girly girl liking horror films."

"I don't think it's weird. It's chocolate and vanilla."

Olivia smiled. "What's that supposed to mean?"

"You know, opinions. One or the other. Some people like vanilla while other people like chocolate."

"And sometimes both," Olivia said.

Michael motioned agreeably. "Exactly. People are gonna like different things. I mean seriously, if everybody in the world all liked the same things, the world would be pretty boring, I think. There would be no diversity."

"I agree. The world needs diversity."

"So, you mentioned that you have a draw to weird phenomenon and stuff like that, hunh?"

Olivia smiled. "Oh absolutely. I always enjoyed reading scary books as a kid. I'd get them at those book fairs we had at school. One of my favorites is Bram Stoker's *Dracula*."

Michael froze for a moment and hoped that Olivia didn't notice. He decided it wouldn't hurt to tell her about the dreams. Besides, he could put a jovial, silly spin on it if it looked like she thought he was nuts and ended it short saying that it's probably nothing. He took a deep breath and started, "Well, then you will love this. I have been having these dreams about this guy who turned out to be a vampire, right?"

Olivia perked up. "Oh, really."

"Yeah, he's trapped in purgatory, and he wants me to get some book called the Nox Noctu something or other to help him get out of purgatory and return to hell or something like that. Weird, hunh?"

"And you are going to do it, Michael."

Michael turned his head toward her in shock. "What… what did you just say?"

Olivia stared intently at Michael. "You will retrieve *The Volumenus Nox Noctis*."

Michael didn't know how to react to what Olivia was saying. "Olivia? Are you all right? You are really freaking me out here!"

Michael noticed a glow in her eyes and then her voice began to change as an evil laugh filled the room. "Michael, Michael. Don't you recognize me?"

Michael stumbled backward and fell against the arm of the couch, "Orrix? What have you done to her?"

Orrix's voice rang out of Olivia, "Be still, Michael. I have only come to give you a message."

"Message? What do you mean?"

"Well, now that you can see my capabilities in your world even though I am trapped in this damn place, perhaps I will stay in this body, hmm?" Olivia began to caress her breasts and move her hands down toward her groin. "I mean look at this body, Michael. What man wouldn't want this?"

Michael shook his head. "You can't—"

"Calm yourself, Michael. Even if I did decide to stay in this body, the life would be drained from her completely in a day's time. I have merely come to tell you that I am close to finding the book and that you need to get ready. I can't have you getting distracted like this. Consider this a warning. If you try and shut me out or lapse in what I am asking you to do, let this serve as a reminder of what I am capable of. If you deny me, I will strike down those closest to you."

"You bastard! You can't do this!"

"Oh, I can't, can I? We shall see about that. Find me the book, Michael, or I will devour your sanity and corrupt your soul." Olivia collapsed forward and Michael caught her.

Olivia's body was limp, and her voice struggled as she began to speak. "Ow! My head! What happened?"

Michael was breathing heavy as he helped her back onto the couch. He needed to think of what he was going to tell her. He couldn't tell her the truth now and risk having her involved in this. "You...you just kinda fainted. Here let me get you a... uh, some water."

Olivia sat with her elbows on her knees, her hands pressed over her face. "How long was I out?"

Michael turned on his way into the kitchen to face her. "It was just for a moment."

"This happened to me last week too. Perhaps I am studying too much to be ready for finals."

Michael froze for a moment at the sink when he realized that Orrix must have visited her before at some point. He turned off the filter he had on the sink and didn't turn to her as he spoke, "Perhaps. Maybe you should go home and get some rest."

Olivia stood up slowly and began to walk toward Michael, who was facing the sink. She placed her arms around him and placed her hands on his chest and began to trace them up and down. "Perhaps you're right. Lead the way."

"Olivia, I really think you should go home and get some rest."

She continued tracing his chest. "It's okay, Mike, I'm okay now. Trust me"

Michael turned to face her. "But are you sure you want to do this, Olivia?"

"Yes, very sure. As sure as I was last weekend. More so actually. I want you, Michael. I want to be close to you, to feel your body against mine."

They went into his bedroom, and after she removed her clothes, she lay down on the bed. Michael noticed that she was wearing a dark satin and lace bra that pushed up her breasts and a pair of panties to match. Michael noticed again how nice her skin looked in the light of the moon coming through the window as he was admiring the curves of her body. He pulled off his pants and shirt then went to lie beside her. They kissed passionately as he caressed her breasts and moved his hand down her thigh, squeezing her flesh. The two gyrated against one another in a dance of mild foreplay. Michael moved on top of her and settled between her hips. She ran her fingers up and down his back and moaned with pleasure as the two connected in a moment of ecstasy.

Later, Michael watched her as she slept while stroking her hair. She was so peaceful and beautiful as if nothing could ever bother her. He watched as she breathed in and out through her nose. Michael focused on how the covers she was under rose and fell. He took his index finger and pushed aside the lock of hair that was lying over her right eye. He traced his fingers across her cheek and down her chin. His index finger felt her lips gently. They were very soft. He kissed her cheek and then lay down with his arms around her to go to sleep. Before he drifted off, he lay there hoping he wouldn't have to see Orrix again tonight. He hoped that after the ordeal he had, he wouldn't have to see him again. Then he started thinking about all that was said that night. About how Michael and those close to him would be punished if he did not do what Orrix had ordered him to do. What else could he do? He knew he would have to help so he could end this whole thing.

CHAPTER 8

Monday, April 23

Later that morning, Michael awoke to see Olivia sitting at the foot of the bed. Her hair was wet, from the shower he assumed, and was just finishing putting her shoes on. Michael gazed across the room and saw the light coming in through the window. It shined down onto the edge of the bed. He moved his hand over into it and smiled at the light's warmth against his skin. Michael looked over at the clock. It was 5:30 a.m.

"Are you leaving?" he said.

"I have a class at eight, so I am gonna go home and put on some fresh clothes."

Michael sat up and placed his hands on her back. "Will I see you later?"

She turned to Michael with a smile. "Maybe." She kissed him and placed her hand on his cheek. Then she stared into his eyes for a moment then stood up and started to walk away when she stopped and turned her head toward him. "Call me later, and maybe we can get together for dinner or something, okay?"

Michael stared at her with emotion-filled weary eyes. "I'll do that."

"So, I'll talk to you later then?"

Michael smiled and giggled slightly as he began to speak, "Yes, you will." Michael continued to stare as she walked out of the room. He listened as she made her way to the front door. After she shut the door, Michael lay down on the bed once more and stared again at the light on his bed. He curled back up in bed under the covers and thought about going back to sleep. He started replaying their time together in his head and breathed out a sigh of contentment. He closed his eyes, and after a few minutes, he fell asleep. He woke up again and wondered what time it was. How long had he been asleep? Looking over at his clock, he saw it was 6:57 a.m. Five minutes later, he got up out of bed and went into the bathroom to shower and get ready for class.

Michael was outside walking toward the building where his first class was. He was staring at the sky, which was a partly cloudy blue sky and was feeling the wind gently blow against him all while thinking about last night. He thought to himself how sappy he must have looked: a stride in his step, staring at the clouds, at the trees, and smiling uncontrollably. He started to think of the image of some romantic film about a young schoolboy who had become infatuated with a fellow schoolgirl. A youth walking aimlessly with nothing but the images and feelings of desire, of passion, and of love, but he knew he was being overcritical of himself and that it would pass. Which, it did when he ran into Tom coming from the other direction.

Michael raised his hand to get Tom's attention. "Hey, Tom, what's up? What are you doing here? Is there no class today or something?"

Tom stopped and stared at Michael with a mixture of disbelief and seriousness. "You mean you didn't hear?"

"Hear what?" Michael felt his weight shifting from his left foot to his right foot, preparing himself for what Tom was going to tell him.

"Mike..." Tom took a deep breath and sighed. "I really don't know how to tell you this, so I am just going to say it... Olivia killed herself this morning. Her dormmate found her in their bathroom."

Michael's eyes grew wide, and his voice struggled to respond, "What? I mean, you're fucking with me right 'cause if you are, this isn't funny, man."

Tom moved closer and put his hand on Michael's shoulder. "I really wish I was, Mike."

Michael felt his head drop. "What, I mean how did—"

Tom interjected, "I don't think you really wanna know that, man, do ya?"

Michael looked up and stared at Tom. "I can handle it. Just tell me."

Tom cleared his throat. "Well, according to what I have been hearing, she slit her wrists while taking a shower. Her dormmate heard the shower running for a lot longer than normal."

Michael's mind began to run in circles trying to put the events together. "This doesn't make any sense." Michael started to mumble to himself quietly. "Her hair, it was wet this morning. It doesn't make any sense." Tom stared at Michael, wondering what he was mumbling about. Then Michael spoke up, "This doesn't make any sense, I mean we were talking about maybe having dinner tonight. Why the fuck would she do that then?" Tom moved in closed and gave Michael a hug. He could hear Michael starting to cry a little and squeezed him a bit harder to reassure him. Michael continued, "How do they know it was really suicide?"

"Well again, I am just going off what I heard, but apparently, her dormmate said that she saw the phrase 'Yes, I can' on the mirror written in what must have been her own blood before she died. They also found a note in the dorm. I don't know what was in that, but it must have been something for someone to have mentioned it. I'm not trying to sound like an ass here, but the whole thing is pretty fuckin' weird if you ask me."

Michael curled his lips in contemplation and decided that it was time to tell someone. "Tom, I am gonna tell you something, and I know you probably aren't gonna believe me, but you just have to. Let's go somewhere else first."

Tom stared at Michael and saw the intent in his face and heard the urgency in his voice. "Mike, what is it? You're freaking me out."

"Just trust me, Tom. C'mon, let's go."

They walked into Michael's apartment, and Tom shut the door. Michael began to speak as they made their way into the kitchen. "Okay, look. Olivia didn't kill herself, she was murdered."

Tom's head leaned back slightly and his eyes squinted. "What! C'mon, get real!"

Michael asserted. "Tom, I'm not kidding."

"Mike, you know how crazy that sounds? Look at the facts, man. There was a note and-and that message on the mirror. I mean seriously. Again, I'm not trying to sound like an insensitive ass here, but I guess she just couldn't handle the pressure this semester. I mean c'mon, even her friends were saying that she was struggling in a few of her classes. You know, it's sad, but it's not unheard of when students can't handle the pressure of college and decide to do things like this. Remember that kid that jumped out of a window from all the pressure three semesters ago? And, hey, look, like I said, I am not trying to come off all insensitive or anything, but—"

Michael interjected, "Tom, you heard that they found her in the shower, right?"

Tom folded his arms across his torso. "Yeah, so?"

"Tom, she was here last night." Michael pointed at the floor for emphasis.

Tom unfolded his hands and moved toward Michael slightly. "What do you mean she was here? Did you two—"

Michael stood without reaction to a question he knew was coming but decided to cut him off once again, "Well, that's not what's important—"

"Holy shit! So, wait, you slept with her, and now she's dead. Oh, man." Tom hesitated for a moment, "You must feel horrible."

Aggravation was growing in Michael, and he snapped at Tom, "That's not the point, Tom!"

Tom instinctively raised his hands up in front of himself, palms out to Michael as if defending himself. "Hey, Mike, look, I mean if I had just slept with someone and then she killed herself the next day, I would be pretty freaked out too, Mikey."

Michael's frustration felt like it was reaching a fever pitch. "Tom! Just listen to me for a minute, okay?"

Tom froze in place and stood staring at Michael. He was very surprised in how excited and angry Michael was getting. "Okay, Mike…okay. I'm listening." Tom sat down.

"Olivia and I went to the movies last night. We came back, and we started talking about weird phenomenon and stuff. She's into that sort of stuff. So, I figured it couldn't hurt to tell her about those dreams I have been having. Plus, she's a psych major who's interested in dreams."

"You mean the dreams you told me about with that guy or figure, right?"

"Yeah, those, just listen. When I finished telling her, she…" Michael stopped and stared at Tom.

Tom's face was the example of anticipation. "What, Mike? She what?"

Michael's voice got quieter as he began to speak, "She-she became possessed by the figure from my dreams and it began talking through her."

That look of anticipation had just turned into utter disbelief. "What!" Tom shook his head to match his face. "Okay, Mike, look, I know this is a blow to you, but—"

"Tom, I am not making this up, okay? This man, this thing, Orrix is real. He's real, and he's a demon, and he wants me to retrieve this book to help him return to hell."

"Wait." Tom's voice was now in total alignment with his face and head. "Return to hell? Why would he want to go back to hell? That makes no sense. Hell is supposed to be this god-awful place where everybody suffers and—"

Michael cut him off and continued to tell his story, "Because that is where he belongs. He's been trapped in purgatory for basically the last century, and now he wants to go back to where he belongs. Look, Tom, you have to believe me. I know this sounds crazy, but you have to believe me!" Michael insisted.

Tom looked down at the floor and shook his head from left to right. "I dunno, Mike, this all sounds really weird, and you are really starting to freak me out here. Are you sure that this isn't—"

Michael's eyes opened wide as he responded, "Yes, Tom! Yes, I am sure! I am so fucking sure it scares me. Look, these are not delusions, they are not visual interpretations of some sort of stress I might be having or any of the symbolic bullshit that people would try to tell me! These are dreams about a fucking demon that wants me to retrieve some book for a purpose that I am still not sure of! And if I don't, according to him, I will be tormented for the rest of my damn life!"

Tom stood up as Michael lowered himself down and squatted on the floor. Tom sat down next to him and placed his hand on Michael's shoulder. "Hey, Mike, it's okay, man…it's okay. Just try to calm down. Let's just relax for a minute."

Michael began to cry. "If you've seen the things I've seen, Tom. The horrors of that place. I don't want to go back there. You have to help me, Tom, please?"

"It's gonna be okay, Mike." Tom was quiet for a moment while Michael composed himself. "So, tell me once more what happened with Olivia. She was possessed by this Orrexo guy?"

Michael was wiping his eyes. "By Orrix, yes."

"So, what does this have to do with her suicide?"

"That's just it. It wasn't suicide. When Orrix was inside of her, he told me that if I didn't help him, he would hurt those closest to me, and I told him that he couldn't do that. So, then he said, 'Oh, I can't, can I?'"

Tom's face filled with horror and disbelief. "Oh my god! That phrase on the mirror!"

"Yes, I can. Don't you see, Tom? I'm not making this up. This is real, and I need your help."

"Okay, Mike. Just tell me what you need me to do. I am here for you, man."

"Thank you, Tom, thank you." Michael and Tom stood up.

"So, you have to get a book for him? What's it called?" Tom asked.

"He said it's called *The Volumenus Nox Noctis*, the book of darkness."

Tom nodded his head. "Okay. So how do we find this book? I mean it could be anywhere."

"He told me it's in some old house off route 34."

"Route 34? That's not exactly a small road."

Michael smirked. "I know. I tried to tell him that too, but when he possessed Olivia, he said he was close to finding it. I just have to wait now."

Tom nodded again. "Okay, so I guess all we can do is wait, right? Mean if you wanted, I can get a car, and we can just drive up and down 34 and see what we see," Tom thought how that idea sounded ridiculous. "Well, I guess that's not a good idea. It would take us forever. Hey, are you sure you are gonna be okay? 'Cause I mean I can stay here if—"

"No. It's okay. I'll be okay. It's just nice to be able to tell someone. You can head back to your place for now if you want. I sort of just want to be alone right now anyway." Tom gave Michael another hug then started for the door when he stopped, turned, and stared at Michael. Michael locked eyes with him and said, "Trust me, I'll be fine."

"All right, but, hey, you just gimme a call if you need anything, all right?"

"Okay. I will talk to you later, and, Tom, thanks, man…"

Tom smiled. "Anytime, bro."

Michael stood in the kitchen as Tom left. He leaned his back up against the counter and placed his hands on the counter's edge. He started thinking of Olivia. Of all the fun they had when they were together as well as the way she made him feel when she was around. He started to think of what had happened last night then found himself trying to shake those thoughts when he began to think about what had happened with Orrix. Images of what probably had happened to her in that bathroom began to flow through his head. He had an image of Orrix in her body staring into the mirror and smiling as he picked up the razor and began to— Michael squeezed his eyes shut hard in an effort to force those thoughts out of his head. Then he started to cry again. He began to mutter under his breath as if trying not to be heard, "You son of a bitch." That night, Michael went to bed hoping for a confrontation.

CHAPTER 9

Thursday, April 26

There were no dreams for Michael last night or the night before that for that matter. Michael wasn't worried because this was something that had happened before. He knew that Orrix would come when he felt the time was right, plus Michael remembered that Orrix said he had waited this long. Part of Michael thought that maybe Orrix was giving him time to think about his actions and get him focused on finding the book. Michael was okay with that as he and Tom were planning on how to handle this house search and what they should bring with them. Michael found himself filled with anticipation and fear for his next encounter with Orrix. It was a strange mix of emotion that Michael simultaneously liked and disliked, which worried him a little. He wanted this to be over as soon as possible so he could get on with his life. He wanted to know Orrix was back where he belonged once and for all. Michael did start to wonder if his life would ever be the same after this whole thing. Would he ever really be able to have a normal life knowing what he knew now?

It was almost 2:30 p.m., Michael grabbed his bag and headed toward his business administration class. Michael had thought about just skipping classes, but he wanted to feel normal so he went.

Tom was sitting down in his chair and straightened up when Michael entered the room. "Hey, Mike! What's up?"

Michael placed his books down and sat down. "Hey, Tom. What's going on?"

"So, did you have another one of those dreams?"

Michael pursed his lips and shook his head. "No, I actually slept last night. It felt good actually. I haven't had a good night sleep for quite some time now."

"Really? That sucks, man. I'm sorry."

"Yeah, well...there was that one night with Olivia..." Michael stared aimlessly ahead toward the front of the classroom as he began to think about Olivia.

"Mike, did you hear me, man?"

Michael refocused and started at Tom. "Hunh? What did you say?"

"I said I can't believe they didn't cancel classes after what happened with her."

"Oh!" Michael shifted in his seat. "Yeah, me too."

"I know it's been a few days, and I have been trying to give you your space, but how are you doing with the whole situation?"

"Well it only happened three days ago, so needless to say, I am still a little shook by the whole thing, but I'm working through it. I don't know if I should be grateful or not, but I dealt with a fair amount of death and loss growing up, so I have learned how to grieve. Jesus, I must sound terrible."

"No man. I understand. But what I meant to ask is, how you are emotionally. I mean I know that you two were starting to get a lot closer."

"Yeah, we were…but like I said, I am processing it all." Michael thought about telling Tom how he truly felt. That he had shed his tears and despite the sadness he felt, he reminded myself that now there was this place in him that Olivia had touched, even if for just a short time, and for that he was eternally grateful. He thought about how his father always told him that sometimes, special people come into our lives for a short time, and even if it saddens us when they go, we have to remember the time we shared and how they touched our lives. Michael thought about saying all that, but for some reason, he decided to keep it to himself. Instead, he simply said, "I just can't wait for this whole thing to be over with really, you know what I mean?"

Tom nodded. "You and me both, Mikey. So, when are the services for Olivia?"

The professor walked in just as Michael began to respond, "Friday night."

After class, Michael and Tom headed to the cafeteria to get some coffee.

"So, what are you doing tonight, Mike?"

"Well, I am trying to keep things normal. So, I am gonna try to finish my paper for McVicker then go to sleep. I just hope I can focus enough to get it done."

"Well if you need someone to talk to, you know I will be up."

"I don't know how you do it sometimes."

"Do what?"

"You barely ever sleep, Tom, and you are never tired."

Tom smiled. "Hey, hey! I sleep. Just in small doses. Seriously, all I need is five to six hours, and I am perfect. Hell, sometimes even if I can get one or two hours, I am set for the day."

Michael sighed. "I wish I didn't have to sleep. Then none of this would have ever happened. Maybe I should have just flaked out on you that night you were at Black Jack's. Then perhaps Olivia would still be alive." His voice began to crack, and Tom noticed a tear that had formed in his left eye.

"Mike. It's okay, man. The sooner we find this book, the sooner this will start to be in our pasts."

Michael cleared his throat. "Yeah…"

"Well…" Tom stood up and put his backpack on. "I'm off. I'll talk to you later. Remember, call me if you need anything."

"Okay, see you later, Tom, thanks."

Later that night in his apartment, Michael stared at his laptop screen. He was trying to finish the conclusion for his paper, but as he predicted, he was unable to focus. He kept thinking about Olivia. Her soft skin, her voice, the tenderness in her kiss, and the gentle caress of her fingers. He looked over into his bedroom and began thinking about the night they shared. For a brief moment, everything disappeared for Michael, everything except Olivia. All he could do now was hope she was in a better place. Michael closed his eyes and shook his head to focus on the paper, but he couldn't. After five more minutes of staring, he shut the lid of his laptop and went to get a soda from the fridge.

Michael sat down and turned on the TV. There was some horror movie on. He wasn't a big fan of horror movies, especially as of late. He tried to take his mind off Olivia, off Orrix as well. He began to think about how disappointing most of these movies were nowadays. The pop star cast, the stupid story about some slasher who was done wrong by the kids in the movie, and the horrible endings they all had. The killers all had a different signature to how they killed their victims. All these ideas were just recycled versions of older ones. He started flipping through the channels, but nothing caught his eye. He shut off the TV and sat on the couch drinking his soda. Michael went to the bathroom then got himself ready for bed. He got under the covers and had a feeling of fear. He shook it off and later fell asleep.

In his dream, Orrix had his back toward Michael. He seemed to float there in an empty dark sky. Then Michael looked down and became surprised when he realized that he wasn't standing on anything at all. He became frightened and began to struggle for balance in the air. He saw spirits floating by. They had no real shape, but he could sense the pain and anguish from them. Michael focused himself and felt the rage he had inside about what had happened to Olivia, of what Orrix had done to her. He felt his hands clench into fists, and his jaw tightened as he clenched his teeth. He braced himself and then spoke.

"Orrix! You son of a bitch! You fucking killed her! I know it was you!" Orrix showed no signs of reaction toward Michael's words. He continued more forcefully this time, "Turn and face me, you asshole! Who the fuck do you think—" Orrix raised his hand and then Michael's voice suddenly faded. He felt as if he had lost his voice. He could only get out a muffled attempt at speaking. Orrix turned to face him then started toward him.

"Shhh, Michael. Quiet now." Orrix's hand was slightly out-stretched in front of him with his palm up as if he was holding a small sphere. "No more talk of this. That whore only distracted you from your task at hand." Michael felt his whole body lurch forward toward Orrix. He wanted to strangle him. To scream in his face how much he hated him. That he wanted him dead, but as he moved forward, Orrix clenched his outstretched hand into a fist and Michael felt his whole body drop to the invisible floor beneath his feet. he looked up and tried to speak through his muffled breath.

"F-fuck…" was all that Michael could muster as he tried to fight through the hold he felt upon him.

Orrix unclenched his fist and lowered his arm. "Yes, yes, I know…fuck me. You, humans, and your colloquial slang. I suggest you leave your anger buried deep within yourself for if you show it to me again, you will regret it."

Michael felt the hold dissipated, and he caught his breath then he stood back up. He thought about saying something else. He felt this sort of obligation from what happened, but then he thought, *What's the point?* He's in control here. Michael knew anything that he could try would be futile. He lamented and started to look around, taking in the surroundings again.

"So, what is this place?" Michael asked. "You keep bringing me to different places."

Orrix paused before responding, "I accept your apology, Michael." The sarcasm in his response was palpable. Orrix continued, "This is the causeway of the lost souls. Most of the other places you have seen until now were the places where both the damned and the lost souls dwell, but in this place, only the lost souls may travel."

"So, how are we here?" Michael asked.

"Well, Michael, I have no soul…and as for you, you aren't really here. It is just a vision that I am showing you."

"Just a vision…but they all seem so real."

"Yes, I know. The sights and the smell, but remember the man in the jungle? Remember what happened when you touched him? Remember the fire? It should have killed you, but since this is merely a vision, you cannot be harmed."

Michael breathed a sigh of relief on hearing that. "Then how do you explain what you did to me?"

"Well I am the one that allowed you to come here, so that means that I can manipulate your soul while you dream, Michael. Enough of that though. The time has come at last. Are you ready to fulfill that which has been asked of you, Michael?"

Michael cleared his throat. "Yes, I am ready."

"Very good. I have had time to gather some more power and reach out further, and I believe I have found it. *The Volumenus Nox Noctis* is in an old house that stands on the grounds of what once was a church. As I told you before, the book had circulated between churches over the years and I believe that its last location was this place and that the book still resides there. Before I was damned, I had learned that it was in this area, and I sensed that it had remained there then. Looks like I was right."

"But where?" Michael asked.

"Walk with me, Michael." Orrix started to walk away on the invisible floor.

Michael watched as the blackness became filled. It was as if scenery was dissolving but in reverse. It was reconstructing itself. Then suddenly, they were in a different place and standing on the ground. They started walking along a path in the woods. The area was grassy and filled with plant life. The trees overhead blocked the rays of the sun from blinding him but shot down through openings in the treetops. Michael stared at the beams of light from the sun. They were so clear to him as they extended down from above and touched the ground.

"Do you recognize this place Michael?"

Michael thought for a moment. "Yeah! Yeah, I do, this is the place where people used to come sometimes to party, but the police busted it up one night after some kid overdosed, and no one has gone back since. You mean the book is in there?"

"Yes, the book is under the floor of the house. A priest from Heinrich and Jacob's clan put it there about one hundred and fifty years ago, and I believe it is still in there. Now this is only a vision of that place. Otherwise, I would have gotten it myself, but *you* must retrieve the book."

Michael thought about how he was going to get there and what he would do once he was there. "Okay, I just need to work out a way to get there and figure out how to," he paused for a moment, "break into this house I guess."

"The details of how are not important to me. You have three days to get me the book, or I shall show you once again the repercussions of your disobedience."

Michael's bottom lip curled in to show his disapproval of the implication and reference from Orrix. Michael replied quickly, "Okay, okay. I'll get it, but what do I do once I have it?"

"When you find the book, you will know what to do."

Michael didn't feel reassured by that answer. "Will I even be able to read it?"

"I think you will find that rather easy once you find it. Now go and find the book and don't worry. Your role in all of this will be over very soon. That I promise."

CHAPTER 10

Friday, April 27

Michael woke up and shot up in bed. He had a sense of excitement in him as he now knew where the book was. His first instinct was to call Tom. He reached over to the side table and picked up his phone to call him. The phone started to ring, but it went to voice mail after four rings, so Michael hung up and called back again. He did this two more times before Tom answered.

"Hello…" Tom answered groggily.

"Tom, it's me, Mike," he said excitedly.

Tom's voice was tired and was struggling to find the energy. "Mike, what's up man? You know it's…its four thirty in the morning, right?"

Michael skipped over the question. "Tom, I know where it is."

Tom sat up in his bed now as well. "What, the book? Are you serious? Where is it?" he asked eagerly.

"Do you remember that old house off Fisher Avenue we heard about where all those people used to party years back?"

"Yeah, you mean the one where that kid died that one night? Off 34 North. So that's where it is, off 34."

"Yup, that's the one."

Tom couldn't believe this, so he asked again. "This book is in *there*?"

"That's what Orrix said. Apparently, it's under the floor of the house."

"Well…okay. So, when do you wanna go get it?"

"He told me I have until Sunday, so how does Saturday sound to you? That should give us time to figure out how to get there and get in. Plus, if it's under the floor, we are gonna need some tools or something."

"Hey, for this I'll break whatever plans there are. I guess Nikki Jenkins will just have to spend the night alone." Tom started to laugh. "Man, I can't believe this is actually happening. I mean we are off to get some ancient book to help a demon. It's fucking wild, man. Are you up for this?" Tom wasn't sure if he was asking Michael or himself.

Michael thought about that for a moment before he replied, "More than ever. I will be so grateful once this is over."

"Me too, Mike. Now try and get some sleep and I'll see you tonight around five so we can head over to the funeral home together. Also, I'll work on getting us a car and some tools for tomorrow. All right, Mike, I'll see ya later." Tom hung up, and Michael lay in bed excited. He wasn't able to go back to sleep for another thirty minutes, but when he did, he slept well.

Later, Tom was sitting in his apartment when he heard a knock on the door. He rose to open it and was greeted by Michael.

"Oh, hey, Mike. C'mon in," Tom said.

Michael walked in. "You ready to go? The viewing starts in forty-five minutes."

"Yeah." Tom closed the door behind him. "Kayla is gonna come meet us here then we are gonna go."

"Oh okay. Hey, how's she doing?" Michael inquired.

"If I am being honest, she is not doing well at all. I guess all of this finally set in. She called me around nine last night. She was crying and talking about how she just can't believe this happened and that they were planning a summer vacation together. I didn't think she should be alone, so I asked her where she was, and she was at her place. I told her that I was coming to pick her up then we went and had some coffee. We stayed there for about two hours and talked. Then I drove her back to her apartment, and we talked some more. You see, they were friends in high school too, so their friendship runs deep."

Michael's eyed widened. "Oh really! Wow. This whole thing must be really hard for her."

"Yeah, but I think she is doing a little better. She just needs to know that she's not alone and there are people around that care about her."

The two turned as they heard a knock at the door.

"That must be her," Tom said. "Mike, can you get my jacket out of my room."

"Yeah, sure." Michael started to walk into Tom's room.

Tom opened the door. "Hey, Kayla," he said as he hugged her. "How are you doing today?" As he pulled away, he could tell that she was crying a little before she came. Her eye makeup looked like it had been smeared then reapplied quickly. Plus, her eyes seemed a little puffy.

"I'm doing all right, thanks, Tom. Last night really helped. Thank you for that," she said. "Now I don't know how I will be once I get there tonight, but you are here, so I can stand by you, right?"

Michael reentered the room. "Hi, Kayla. How are you?"

"Oh, Mike!" She walked over and hugged Michael. "How are you doing?"

"I'm doing okay, I guess. I just... I just can't believe all this actually happened, you know?"

Kayla nodded his head while frowning slightly. "Yeah, I know what you mean," Kayla replied. "She was kinda stressing about her classes, and I know she was worried about getting enough money for our summer trip, but I never thought it was all getting to her this badly. I mean I have known her for almost seven years, but I never knew she was hurting this badly. All the time we spent together, I just never saw this coming."

Michael nodded. "Yeah."

"I just..." Kayla's voice went silent as she started to cry. "I just never thought she would do something like this. I'm just shook over the whole thing."

Tom came over and hugged her from the side while leaning his head onto hers, hoping that by doing so she would know that he was there for her.

Michael briefly thought about telling her about Orrix and what actually happened. He thought in some weird way that it would give Kayla some closure, but he knew that she would either become even more upset or not even believe him. He felt that it was best to just not say anything. He paused for a moment as he thought about what to say. He felt like he had to say something. "Well, sadly, I have had to experience loss a bunch growing up. An aunt, two grandparents, cousins, friends, and even some pets. I can say that despite how prepared one can be, death is always a surprise, and when it happens like this, it's hard to know how to feel. You want answers, but there's none to be found, so you feel sort of lost. But like Tom said, we're here for you. You don't have to go through this alone. That's important to remember even when you feel you have hit bottom or are lost in sadness."

Kayla smiled through her tears as she tried to stop them from messing up her makeup again. "Thank you. Thank you both. I know we don't know each other really well, but that means a lot to me." She dabbed her tears a bit more then took a breath. "Perhaps we should get going?"

Michael nodded then looked at Tom. "You know how to get there, right?"

Tom nodded. "Leave it to me Mike."

They walked into the funeral home, and everyone was in a line waiting to approach the casket. Michael noticed all the flower arrangements that hung from the walls and some that were sitting on the floor around the walls. There were two large photo collages that had been made and placed up side by side. They were pictures of Olivia when she was young all the way up till now. Michael noticed one in particular. It was Olivia with her father. Olivia was on his shoulders at the beach. She couldn't have been more than ten years old in that picture. He noticed how bright it seemed wherever they were in that photograph. The smile that was on her face made him think of how he used to make her smile. They looked so happy in that picture. He found himself smiling as well.

Michael was finally up near the casket. It was open, and he looked at Olivia as he waited for the others to finish paying their respects so he could go up next. When it was his turn to walk up, he felt as if his feet were nailed to the floor. He felt the tightness move up his stomach until it filled his throat, and he felt a single tear fall from his right eye. He made his way up toward the casket. He stared for a brief moment, noticing how artificial her skin looked, but despite that, she still looked beautiful and peaceful. He knelt down on the small padded bar and lowered his head. He made the sign of the cross upon himself and began to pray.

"God, if you can hear me, please, God, let Olivia be at peace in heaven. Please, don't let her end up anywhere else." Michael dreaded the idea that she could be in purgatory or somewhere worse. He continued his silent conversation, "Olivia…please, forgive me. This is all my fault. I should have never gotten so close to you when I knew this thing was going on. You didn't deserve this. Please, forgive me?" Michael stood up and wiped his face of tears and made his way toward Olivia's immediate family. Standing there were her two brothers, her mother, and her father was at the end. He walked up to each person, and one by one, he gave his condolences. He stopped at her father and began to speak with him. "Mr. Jackson, I am very sorry for your loss. I knew Olivia from college, and she was truly a great person."

Olivia's father smiled a little. "Well, thank you for saying that. That's very kind of you. Just remember Olivia lives on forever now in our minds and in our hearts." Olivia's father placed his hand on Michael's shoulder and gave a firm squeeze and nodded his head with another small smile.

Michael shook his hand then made his way back to where Tom and Kayla were sitting. Everybody was beginning to sit down. Olivia's father and a priest were standing at the podium up front waiting for everyone to find a seat. After all were seated, the priest began to speak.

"When death comes to us like a thief in the night, we are left with nothing but shattered emotions and the memories of our dearly departed. But in these times of trouble, we must turn to God for guidance." The priest paused for a moment then continued, "Olivia Jackson has touched us all in her own way, and though she is no longer with us in form, she will continue to live on in our minds and in our hearts. In spite of death, she will live on inside of us, and she will not die. We must remember that death is not the end for those who believe in Christ. It is when the soul returns to God. Mr. Jackson has asked me to read a passage for Olivia, and I would like to do that now. Let us pray."

Many people in the room lowered their heads. Michael did the same.

"The Lord is my shepherd, I shall not want. He maketh me to lie down in green pastures, he leadeth me beside the still waters. He restoreth my soul, he leadeth me in the paths of righteousness for his name's sake. Yea, though I walk through the valley of the shadow of death, I will fear no evil for thou art with me, thy rod and thy staff they comfort me. Thou preparest a table before me in the presence of mine enemies, thou anointest my head with oil, my cup runneth over. Surely goodness and mercy shall follow me all the days of my life, and I will dwell in the house of the Lord forever... At this time, I will ask all of us to observe a moment of silence and pray for our dearly departed, Olivia."

Michael closed his eyes. He began to think about Olivia and hoped again that she wouldn't have to go to that place of horrors where he had been so many times in his dreams. Then he began to ask for forgiveness. Tears began to form in his eyes once again. All kinds of thoughts began to form in his mind. "She's dead because of me. I am to blame. If I never told her about this whole thing, Orrix would have never done this. If I just got that damn book sooner, this would be over. and she would still be here. You are going to pay, Orrix."

After the wake, Mike and Kayla returned to Tom's place. Michael was sitting on a chair near the kitchen. Tom and Kayla were sitting on the couch. Tom put his arm around Kayla. "Can I get you anything?"

Kayla was wiping tears from her face. "No, I am okay. I just can't believe she's gone."

Tom called over, "Mike, would you grab me a box of tissues?"

Michael nodded his head. "Yeah, sure, no problem." He stood up and began to walk to the bathroom when a vision flashed in his mind. He came to a sudden stop and shook his head. He wasn't quite sure what the vision was of. The image flashed so fast that he couldn't make it out. He continued forward to the bathroom to get the tissue. He halted again. Another vision. The only thing he could make out was blood and tears. He moved to the sink and turned on the taps. He splashed some water on his face and stared at the mirror for a moment, centering himself. He dried his face and then returned back to the living room with the tissues. "Here you go."

Kayla replied, "Thanks, Mike. You know, this might be a bad time, but Olivia liked you a lot, Mike. She told me after we went to Black Jack's that she thought you were a great guy. When we met the next day, she told me that despite an odd ending to the evening, she felt there was potential. Then you two started hanging out, and she seemed really happy. I just thought you should know that even though you two knew each other for a short time, you had a positive impact on her."

A tear fell from Michael's eye, but he wiped it fast. "Thank you, Kayla. That is really nice to hear." He paused for a moment and exhaled a deep breath in the hopes that his tears would stop. "Are you sure you are going to be okay?"

Kayla nodded and then looked at Tom and placed her hand on his knee. "Yeah, I think so. It is going to take some time, but Olivia will always be a part of me. It's like the priest said, she will be in my thoughts and in my heart forever."

At eleven thirty, Michael headed back to his apartment. He sat on his bedside thinking about how tomorrow he and Tom would go recover *The Volumenus Nox Noctis* for Orrix, then this would all be behind him. Orrix would be back in hell where he belongs, and the natural balance of things would be back to where they once were. Then Michael started to think about how even if Orrix did return to hell, wouldn't he still be set loose on earth again to turn humans into vampires? What if Orrix turned him into a vampire or just killed him? Or perhaps Satan would know he escaped and just destroy him for leaving the place he was damned to. Or maybe he would get sent right back.

Michael wondered what would come next, but selflessly, he just wanted his part in this to be over. He knew he had to do this. He didn't see how it could get worse. Look how far things had come, and Orrix threatened worse if he refused to help. Michael couldn't live with himself if another person got hurt. He knew that no matter what happened to him, he had to do this even if it killed him. He surprised himself that he had come to accept that he might not come back from this. Michael lay down fully dressed and let his acceptance and realization sink in. In ten minutes, he was asleep.

CHAPTER 11

Saturday, April 28

Michael awoke with the light of the sun shining down on his face from the window across the room. It shot through the panes of glass and crawled across the floor up onto his bed. His weary eyes opened and shut suddenly as they tried to adjust to the brightness of the sun. His mouth was dry and his body felt weak. He rose up and placed his hands over his eyes and began to rub them. His fingers traced down his face as his arms fell to the bed. He exhaled slowly and turned his head to the window to note that it was certainly morning. He swung his legs over the edge of the bed. He hunched over as he breathed slowly then placed his feet onto the floor and made his way into the bathroom. On his way to turn the stereo on, he noticed that his shoes were off; he thought that he must have kicked them off in the middle of the night. His body felt stiff now as he walked some more. He began to think how good a warm shower would feel.

He turned on the shower faucet and began to take off his clothes. The room began to fill with steam. The stereo was play-ing rock music in the background. The sounds of the guitars and drums echoed off the shower walls as he stepped into the shower and shut the glass door. The water sprayed down on his face and trickled down to his chin. The water felt good as it hit his skin. He closed his eyes and opened his mouth as he felt the water trickle into his mouth. He spit it out slowly. Michael reached for the soap when suddenly he felt an agonizing pain in his head. He let out a scream of pain and grabbed at his skull. He leaned back against the wall holding his head with one hand while supporting himself with the other. The pain came again, and this time, he fell to his knees in the shower as the pain pierced through his skull. Then he heard a voice that made his chest tighten and caused him to become short of breath. The pain was so intense that he couldn't make out everything that was being said in his mind. He tried to block out the pain so he could understand the words flowing through his mind.

"Michael…be…ou…ust…ot…rix. He…ill…srtoy…Do… go."

Michael's hands were on either side of his head now, pressing his palms on his temples. Then the pain left him, and he rolled to his side and took in deep breaths. He coughed violently as the tears of pain that were running from his eyes were now mixed in with the water from above. He began to think that it was Orrix playing games with him, but he knew even after all he had seen and experienced with Orrix that even he could never cause such a feeling of pain and helplessness. Or could he? He tried to rise to his feet but began to fall again. His left shoulder slammed against the tile wall, and he laid his hand against the glass door. He took another slow breath and began to rise again. He placed his hands against the wall and lowered his head. The water now felt as if it was slamming against his skin. He turned and shut off the shower. He opened the door and stepped out.

As soon as his feet hit the rug, he fell forward to the floor again as the voice entered his head again. He screamed so loud that he couldn't even hear the stereo in the next room anymore. Blood began to drip from Michael's nose as the voice began to communicate again.

"Michael...hav...fear...help...ou...w...shall...meet... oon."

The words were fractured in his mind. Whimpers of pain escaped from his body like a child that had just been physically scolded from its parent. He lay there naked on the floor crying, and then he began to speak aloud to himself. His voice was filled with pain and frustration.

"Why is this happening to me? Why don't you just leave me the hell alone? I can't take any more of this!" He continued to lie there for a moment then sat up and wiped the tears from his face. He wasn't sure what was going on now. Perhaps Orrix was trying to make sure he followed through with what he had promised he would do. "You'll get your fucking book, you fucking asshole!" Michael grabbed a towel and headed back into his bedroom to get dressed.

Michael walked into the kitchen and grabbed a can of soda from the refrigerator. He opened the can and took a big sip. He made his way over to the counter and placed down the can of soda. He stared at his phone for a moment then picked it up to call Tom. It rang twice before Tom answered.

"Hello?"

"Tom? It's Mike"

"Hey. Mike, what's up? You okay? Is something wrong?"

Michael heard those words echo in his head for a moment.

Is there something wrong?

Tom heard nothing. "Mike? You there?"

Michael gathered his thoughts and responded. "Yeah, I'm here. Hey, I was wondering you want to meet up, and I don't know go get some food or something so we can talk about our plan for tonight? Jesus, that sounds weird."

"Well, it's safe to say that this whole situation is pretty freakin' weird, Mike, but yeah, that sounds like a good idea. You wanna meet at the diner? I could go for a salsa chicken sandwich."

Michael laughed. "Dude, how can you eat that shit?" Michael thought how good it felt to laugh. "The diner sounds good though. How soon can you be there?" Michael could hear that Tom was stretching as he started to reply.

"Well, give me twenty minutes here, I have to do some hygienics and then I'll be on my way. So, make it forty-five. Sound good?"

"Yeah, okay, I will see you there."

"Okay. Later, Mike."

"See ya."

Michael ended the call and continued drinking his soda. Twenty minutes later, he headed out to the diner. Michael walked into the diner and was greeted by the manager, Jack. Tom and Michael were regulars, so they knew most of the staff at the diner. Because of this, Jack would just let them seat themselves. Michael sat in a booth near the front window so he could see Tom when he came. After a few minutes, Tom was walking up the sidewalk as the busboy brought the water out. Michael nodded to the busboy to thank him for the water. Tom walked in, and Michael raised his arm to signal to him.

"Hey, Tom."

"What's up, Mike?" Tom replied.

The waitress came over and placed down two menus. Michael raised his hand slightly as if to reject the menus.

"No, thank you, I'm not ordering anything to eat. I'll just have a coffee, please," Michael said as he fidgeted with the fork on his napkin.

The waitress looked over to Tom. "Anything for you, sweetie?"

Tom smiled. "Oh yes, I'm starvin'. Can I have the salsa chicken sandwich with fries and a cup of coffee?" Tom looked at the table and noticed an empty small white bowl. "Oh yeah, we are gonna need some creamers here also please."

The waitress wrote down their order then looked up. "All right. Anything else?"

Michael shook his head. "Nope."

Tom looked up at the waitress. "Yeah, that's all. Oh wait, can I get some gravy on my french fries? Thank you."

"Gravy on the fries. Okay. Thanks, guys. Be right back with your coffee." The waitress turned and walked toward the kitchen.

Michael smiled and shook his head. "Jesus, Tom. You eat the worst food."

Tom smirked. "Yeah, yeah, I know. I like to think that my heart and stomach would like a challenge."

The waitress brought over their coffee and some extra creamers. "Here you go, guys."

Michael shook his head in wonderment. "You seriously can't keep eating like this. I mean ever since I've known you, all you eat is greasy food."

"Yeah, yeah, I know, I'll be dead by morning. Now pass the sugar."

Michael was quiet while they both added sugar and cream to their coffee. Michael was stirring his coffee when he started to speak. "So, what time do you want to meet up tonight to do this?"

Tom tapped his spoon on the lip of his cup to shake off the excess coffee before placing it down. "Shit, Mikey, you don't waste much time, do you?"

"Well, excuse me. I'm sorry if I want to get this damn thing over with. I mean it's not like you been having these dreams with this asshole in them!"

Tom shifted in his seat. "Hey, Mike, take it easy. You keep talking like that, and people are gonna start looking over here."

Michael looked down at the table and held his cup of coffee with both hands. "I'm sorry, it's been a rough morning. Besides, when are you the kinda person who doesn't like getting attention?"

"Well, girls can't dig a guy while he is eating."

Michael look at Tom quizzically. "What?"

"No seriously. You ever notice how disgusting and animalistic people look when they eat? It's such a turn off. I mean c'mon. Pick any attractive person, and I bet you they look nasty when they eat. I mean look at the salad. Healthy, but there's no way anyone looks attractive when they eat a salad."

Michael was just shaking his head. "You're too much, man, but you know something..." Michael envisioned someone eating a salad, the large piece of lettuce covered in dressing at the end of the fork. The person opening their mouth wide trying to fit the large bite in their mouth. "You actually have a point there."

Tom raised his coffee cup, smiling in acknowledgement that he was right, then he took a sip. "I know. Anyway, back to this morning. So, did something happen? Is that why you're stressed out, I mean aside from all the other weird shit that has been happening?"

"Well…yeah, Orrix came to me while I was in the shower. I could hear this voice in my head, and he was trying to tell me something, but I couldn't make out what he was saying. Probably because I was in so much pain, and honestly, the whole thing felt different to me, but it had to be him."

"What? So, wait, he was talking to you, where? In your head?"

"Yeah, I had this pain in my head and a tightness in my chest. Orrix was talking to me, but I was in so much pain I couldn't really make out what he was saying, and it didn't really sound like him, but again, I was in the shower and my head was pounding."

Tom leaned in. "What do you think he was trying to tell you?"

"Probably the same thing he's always talking about." Michael began to speak in a deeper tone of voice, "Bring me the book, Michael, or I will make sure you suffer for *all* eternity." Michael returned his voice to normal pitch. "He is probably just making sure I go through with this. A warning perhaps, but there was just…" Michael paused as he leaned back in his seat, "…something."

"What?" Tom asked.

Michael was staring up at the ceiling. "There was just something different about it this time."

Tom placed his coffee down onto the table. "Hey, you said yourself this Orrix guy is an asshole." Tom began to yawn but kept talking, "I am sure he is just messing with you again.

But don't worry, we are gonna end this thing once and for all. Whaddya say I meet you at your place around nine?"

Michael nodded. "All right. That sounds good."

"Okay." Tom started looking around the diner. "Where the hell is my food? Hey, what's our waitress's name?"

Michael shook his head. "I don't know."

Tom elevated himself slightly in his booth and turned toward the front counter where their waitress was sitting outside smoking a cigarette. Tom got up and went to knock on the window. "Hey, waitress!" Michael couldn't help but smile when he thought about how blunt and inconsiderate Tom could be sometimes.

Later that night back at his apartment, Michael was sitting on the couch waiting for Tom to arrive. He had a can of soda resting on the table. His feet were tapping nervously on the floor as he stared off into the distance. His eyes focused on nothing in particular as he sat thinking of what had to be done this evening. He couldn't sit still, so he stood up and began to pace back and forth in his apartment. His eyes now fixed at the floor as he walked from one end of the room to the other. He breathed in and out through his nose, constantly thinking of Orrix and the book. He looked at the clock on the microwave in the kitchen, 8:56 p.m. He made his way back the other way and was just about to sit back down on the couch when he found himself thinking of Olivia. Of how they sat on that couch and held each other, but that memory was shattered when he remembered how Orrix ruined it all with his trickery.

There was a knock at the door. It was Tom.

"Hey, Mike you there? Mike?"

Michael made his way to the door. He undid the dead bolt and removed the chain from the door.

Tom was smoking a cigarette all dressed in black. "You ready to go, Mike?" He looked at Michael's clothes. "Wait, you are gonna wear *that*?"

Michael looked down at his shirt. "What's wrong with my shirt?"

Tom held out his hands at his side. "Dude, it's kind of bright. We are sneaking into a house, do you want someone to see us?"

Annoyed, Michael shook his head. "Okay, okay, I'll change it." Michael walked into his bedroom, changed his shirt to a solid heather-black T-shirt and returned with a black-hooded sweatshirt as well. He locked the door, and they left. They made their way downstairs and into the car that Tom had gotten from some ride share app. They were driving in complete silence for a while. Michael was looking at the road when it seemed as if Tom was about to speak but changed his mind. Michael didn't really feel like talking anyway. He was focused on finding the book. They made a left onto Route 34 to head toward Fisher Avenue. The silence was broken when Michael began to speak. "Tom?"

"Yeah, Mike?"

"Look…if something happens in there, I don't want you to be brave and try to save me. I-I just want you to save yourself."

Tom rolled his eyes. "Mikey, nothing is going to happen to you while—"

Michael cut him off, "Look, when we find this book, just be sure to stand back. Orrix said I would know what to do when

I found the book, and I don't know what will happen. So, just promise me you will run if something happens."

"Mike...seriously? Do you really expect me to just—"

Michael insisted, "Tom, just promise me, okay?"

Tom looked over at Michael and saw how serious he looked. Tom couldn't help but think about how unbelievable this all seemed. "Okay. Okay, Mike, you got it. If something happens, I'll run." Tom's voice filled with sarcasm. "I won't try to be a hero. I'll run just like you said. I promise."

"Thanks, Tom." Michael looked down at his phone. "The GPS says that Fisher Avenue is the third left comin' up."

Tom had a solemn tone in his voice now. "Yeah, okay."

They made the left onto Fisher Avenue and headed down the road to the old house on the right.

"Not much of a road is it, Mike?"

Michael stared out the window. "Well, we are out in the boonies."

"So, this place is deserted now, right?" Tom asked.

"I don't think anyone has lived here for like ten years, so yeah, you could say that."

"Yeah, that's true. So, what about all these other houses?"

"They were probably bought up by some company who wanted the land. I guess they wanted to tear them down and rebuild. Probably another strip mall with a coffee shop or something. Or maybe it will be one of those gated communities."

"How do you know that?" Tom slowed the car down, and Michael pointed over to a construction company sign. "Oh."

Michael pointed ahead. "Hey, there it is up on the right."

"I see it." Tom parked the car in the driveway. He turned off the motor, and they sat there for a moment. They both stared straight ahead at the house.

"You ready, Mike?"

Michael sat there motionless, still staring at the house.

Tom turned to face Michael. "Mike?"

Michael turned to face him quickly with wide eyes. "Hunh?"

"You okay?"

"Yeah, I'm fine. Let's go."

Tom shrugged his shoulders. "Okay."

They got out of the car and met up at the rear of the car. Michael noticed how the moon was shining down and lit up the surroundings with its luminescence. It was a clear night. The wind moved gently through the trees, causing the branches to shake. Michael couldn't help but think of how the undulation of the wind through the trees made it sound like the ocean.

"Not much around here anymore, hunh, Mike?"

Michael replied, "No, not really." Tom opened the trunk of the car, and Michael looked in. He stared confused then looked at Tom. "Crowbars? The tools you said you were gonna get are just two crowbars?"

Tom looked at Michael, almost as if insulted. "What? Hey, man, you can do almost anything with a crowbar. It's a wonderful tool. Wanna open a door? Crowbar. Need a window opened? Crowbar. Some asshole gets all up in your shit? Crowbar. Besides, I figured it would look suspicious if I bought two shovels, two axes, or some tools like that. Besides, they were just twelve bucks a piece, and I got two flashlights."

Michael shook his head in astonishment at Tom's reasoning. "Okay, man." The two picked up the crowbars and flashlights. Tom shut the trunk then turned toward Michael.

"You ready to go in?" Tom asked.

"Yeah. You?"

Tom steeled himself. "Yup."

"Okay, let's go and remember—"

Tom rolled his eyes. "I know, I know. No hero business."

Michael nodded. They both hesitated for a second then started to walk toward the front porch. The house had two floors. They noticed that there were broken windows in the front, and despite the darkness, they could see the paint of the house was peeling and had some graffiti in some sections. Michael looked over the windows and saw only two that were intact. Suddenly, Michael froze in his footsteps as the pain in his head returned. Tom turned to him as Michael dropped his flashlight and grabbed at his head.

"Mike? Hey, Mike, are you all right?"

Michael let out a sigh of pain. "My head. My god it hurts." Another sigh of pain quickly escaped. Tom moved quickly toward Michael.

"Mike? Mike! What should I do?"

Michael's hearing was starting to fade out. He looked up and stared at Tom and only saw his lips moving. It sounded as if someone had turned the volume on a stereo all the way up, but nothing was playing. There was just this loud static hiss that was drowning out everything around him.

Tom was getting really worried. "Mike? Mike? Can you hear me? Jesus! Mike!"

Michael began to feel a tightness in his chest, and he fell to his side. He then heard the voice in his head again.

"Michael…ou…must…go…in…must…ook…"

The voice was unclear and didn't stay long like before. Michael found himself lying on his back with Tom screaming his name, but he was cut off as Michael began to scream.

"Orrix! You are gonna get your damn book! I'm here! What more do you want from me!"

Tom stood there in silence staring at Michael. He had never seen Michael so enraged. "Hey, Mike?" He stepped closer and leaned down toward Michael and extended his hand and was about to place it on Michael's shoulder when he turned quickly to face Tom. He was breathing heavy, and his eyes were filled with anger. Tom flinched and moved back slightly. "Mike, it's me. Are you okay?"

Michael was breathing slower now with his eyes closed. "Yeah, I'm okay. It was…just Orrix again."

Tom let out a sigh of relief. "Jesus Christ! You scared the shit outta me!"

"I know… I know, I'm sorry, I'm okay now." Tom just stared at him. "Really, I'm okay now."

"You're sure?" Tom asked.

Michael nodded. "Yeah, let's just go inside." Tom helped Michael up.

They opened the door and walked inside. They both cringed as they took in the dank air that filled the entryway. Michael noticed how dark it seemed at the end of the hallway. The rest of the area was dark as well, and there was dirt across the floorboards that lead into one of the rooms. The moon shined in from the windows, and the wood creaked as they walked in.

"Oh man, this place smells." Tom waved his hand in front his face a few times. "Well, where should we start looking, Mike?"

Michael was scratching at the back of his head. "I don't know. Let's try over there. Hey, shut the door."

Tom shut the door, and they headed toward what appeared to be the dining room off to the right. As their flashlights panned the floor, they noticed how repugnant the carpet was. There were insects moving around in the fabric and water stains scattered across it. There was dirt and dust just about everywhere. They noticed empty beer cans and bottles off in the corner and on the end of one table. There were spots of candle wax also melted on to the table. Tom moved forward and looked down at a mound of what appeared to be old, dried vomit. The smell of the room made him cringe and left him with a sick feeling in his stomach.

"Oh man, Mike. This place is fucking filthy!"

"Yeah, you can say that again." Michael continued shining the flashlight around the room looking for something. But for what exactly, he didn't know.

Tom giggled. "This place is fucking filthy! Jesus, I don't know where to look, Mike. Do you…you feel anything or what?"

"I don't know." Michael said as he continued to look around. "I thought Orrix would have given me a sign or something."

Michael started to move forward and then stopped as he felt a feeling of warmth in his hands, followed by a ringing in his head. Then a voice called out to him.

"Michael." It was clear this time. It was Orrix. "Michael. Go down the hall, Michael."

Michael shook his head, agreeing to the voice in his head. He turned to head back towards the entryway and then looked down the hall. His eyes opened wide.

Tom turned as Michael started walking out of the room. "Mike? You all right, man?"

Michael had already started down the hallway. "Yeah." His voice was slightly louder than a whisper, "Let's go this way."

Tom followed him. As they walked down the hall, Tom noticed the wallpaper that was on the walls. Parts of it were torn off. Other parts had spray paint on them. One part read "Bill Loves Marnie."

Michael turned to Tom and began to speak. His voice seemed excited, "Hey, Tom, this must have been the living room. Look at the desk and the couches. There's a fireplace over there."

"You think it's in there? At least this room doesn't have insect-infested carpets, but I'll bet this place has termites."

"Yeah, you're probably right. Hey, you see a light switch anywhere?"

"Yeah, here we go." Tom flipped the switch, and nothing happened. "I don't know why I thought that would work. Okay, Mike. Now what?"

"I should have figured that would have happened. Let's look around. The book has to be here somewhere. Look for loose floorboards or something. Orrix said it was buried under the floor."

Tom snickered. "What like in the Hardy Boys? Sure thing, Frank."

The irritation was growing in Michael. "C'mon, man, stop fooling around."

"Hey, I'm sorry, man, but this place is kinda creepy. I feel like some freak in a mask is gonna pop out any minute. Besides, I joke around when I get nervous, you know that."

Tom noticed that Michael's voice now had signs of irritation as he replied. "Yeah, whatever. Just help me look."

Tom nodded in agreement and began to look around the floor for something strange. After five minutes of looking, Tom was starting to get frustrated too. "Hey, look, Mike, I dunno where this damn book is. Maybe we should go look somewhere else." Tom stared at Michael. "I'm gonna go look upstairs." Michael didn't seem to hear him as he was lost in his thoughts looking for the book. "Mike? Mike!"

Michael turned quickly to face Tom with a look of surprise. "Hunh? What?"

"I am gonna go look upstairs!"

"Uh yeah, okay. Just call me if you need me."

Tom was already walking out of the room. "Yup."

Michael moved over toward the fireplace and began to look in the flue. He started thinking how silly all this seemed. He walked over to a desk that was against the far wall. He began to search the drawers for the book. There was nothing in them really. Some used condoms and cigarette butts and some other junk. Then he remembered to check the floor. So, he placed his flashlight down on the desk and started to push it across the floor. It creaked a little and made a loud scratching sound as it slid across the floor. He examined the floor and didn't see anything unusual. He sat down on top of the desk and exhaled with a great sigh. He was also now starting to get frustrated looking for the book.

"Mike!" Tom's voice echoed throughout the house. Michael sat up, and his eyes opened wide with alarm. He stood up quickly and began running toward Tom's voice. "Mike, I think I found it. I think I found it!"

Michael yelled as he ran back down the hall, "I'm coming!" He turned and raced up the stairs two at a time. Then he met Tom at the top of the steps. "What did you find? Where is it?"

Tom was on his knees trying to pull up a board with his crowbar. "This board seemed looser than the others when I walked on it."

"Hey, it's worth a shot. Move over." Michael said as he kneeled down and instinctively grabbed the exposed end of the board with his palms up as they began to try and pry up the board. The board came up halfway then got stuck from the nails in it. Michael pushed up as hard as he could, but he couldn't get it. He let go and exhaled a mixture of annoyance and defeat. "Hey, gimme the crowbar." Michael said. Tom handed it to him and watched as he jammed it under the side of board and started to shimmy it under further. "Look out." Tom moved aside as Michael squatted, gripped the crowbar with both hands and started to lift as hard as he could, then the board snapped, and the crowbar hit Michael in the chest. He stumbled forward and was groaning.

Tom moved toward him. "You all right?"

Michael was rubbing his chest. "Yeah, the fucking crowbar caught me in the chest, but I'm okay."

Tom knelt down and began to feel around underneath the floorboards. "There is a lot of dust and shit under here." He continued to feel around, "Oh, man, I don't wanna know what that is." He continued to feel around then paused suddenly. "Mike, there's a book under here!"

"Holy shit! Well stop jerking off and get it."

"I'm trying, but my arms only go so far." Tom stretched out as far as he could. "Got it." Tom removed his arm from under the floor and pulled out a book wrapped in cloth. "Here you go."

Michael took it from him and quickly removed the cloth. Once the book was exposed, he turned it around inspecting its features. "It looks kinda…plain."

Tom stood up wiping the dust off his shirt. "What were you expecting, Mike? A book bound in human flesh and inked in blood?"

Michael just gave him a somewhat disappointed stare then began to speak, "Well I thought a book like *The Volumenus Nox Noctis* would have been something a little more… I don't know creepy. I mean this is just a blue book, and how do we know that this is it? I mean there's no title on it or anything like that."

"This isn't a movie, Mike. Sometimes things are just plain and simple. Besides, this has to be it. Why else would there be a book hidden under the floorboards?"

"Yeah, you're right. I don't know what it is really. I guess in a way a part of me was all built up about this moment."

"Yeah, well, so what do we do now?" Tom asked.

Michael stared at the book and shrugged his shoulders slightly. "I don't know."

They both began to walk downstairs as Michael opened the book and began flipping through the pages. He noticed pictures of what appeared to be angels that had lost their wings. He noticed one in particular with dark hair and a look of anger and resentment in his eyes. He figured that had to be Satan. He tried to read the writing, but it was written in a strange language that he did not know.

"Hey, Tom, look at this. It has drawings of angels and what appears to be a fallen angel. I can't read the writing though. I don't know what is supposed to happen. Orrix said I would know what to do. Perhaps we should just take it and go."

"It's Aramaic."

Michael looked up at Tom. "What did you say?"

"The book, Michael..." Tom turned toward Michael. Michael noticed a strange look in his eyes. He knew he had seen it somewhere before. "It's written in Aramaic."

Michael took a few steps back and held the book against his chest. "Oh my god! Tom, is that you?"

"A piece of him, Michael. I must congratulate you. I really couldn't have done this without you."

"Orrix! What have you done to Tom?" Michael's voice echoed off the walls of the house.

"The same as I did to Olivia that evening in your apartment. I am borrowing him temporarily. Just long enough to suit my needs."

Michael shook his head from side to side. "Your needs, but why?"

"Why? Because I cannot allow the Matheson descendant to live, that's why."

Michael began to back away from him as he moved closer. "You mean you are going to kill me?"

Tom stopped walking. "You? No. Thomas here, yes."

Michael froze and stood wide-eyed. "What did you say?"

"Michael, do you really think you were strong enough to get here on your own? I knew you would bring Thomas to me. After all, he was too strong for me to go to directly. I needed time to harness the power to do this, and I would never be able to maintain that power in my current state against a Matheson, so I decided to take an alternate route, the weak friend." Orrix began to laugh.

Michael shook his head in disbelief. "You-you—"

"Yes, yes, I know. What can I say, Michael, I lied. You have absolutely no relation to Heinrich, but I knew a person like you would believe it, and I know you understand what I mean. You feel it even now, don't you? That feeling of no identity, of no direction, it's that overwhelming feeling of not knowing where your place is in this world. That's exactly what has made you come this far. I mean with my presence, with this task, you finally had that feeling of purpose."

Michael just stood shaking his head from left to right. "You are trying to mess with my head. It won't work."

Orrix began to laugh again as he resumed walking toward Michael. "But it has worked, Michael. Why do you think you are here? It was Thomas who descended from the Matheson blood-line. He is the last, and now he is going to die, but not before he helps me return to where I belong." Orrix snatched the book from Michael's hands. Michael looked into Orrix's eyes, which were now fiery red, and the fear in him told him to turn and run, but it was as if his body would not respond. Orrix was flipping through the book. "Now let's see...ah, here we go."

Michael was standing there staring at Orrix now possessing his best friend when he tightened his fists and straightened up. He began to open his mouth to speak. "Please, Michael—" Orrix struck him across the face and Michael fell to the floor. "No interruptions."

Michael watched as Orrix let go of the book, but it did not fall. It seemed to hover there in front of him. It was then that Orrix began to speak. "When Lucifer lost his battle to the Lord, he was cast down into the farthest depths which we now know as hell. In his rage, he decided that even though he had lost his battle against God, he would not stop fighting for what he believed. Lucifer had dominion over all the realms of hell, and God had control of all the realms of heaven. In his power, God decided to create a realm of waiting for those who had lost their way or had committed some of the greatest sins. It would be a place of redemption through purification. This realm became to be known as purgatory. It is a place of pain and suffering for the damned and a place of waiting for the lost souls. The passages recorded here were given to the Archangel Gabriel from the Lord and passed onto the angel of death to be recorded in this book. On the recitation of these passages, a soul can be liberated from the prison known as purgatory."

Michael sat up against the wall near the steps in wonderment. He watched as Orrix walked over toward the hallway and began to read again. This time, Michael heard Toms voice. "And the damned shall be sent to the realm of waiting. Those damned souls shall suffer there for a time determined by God. When the time of suffering has ended, they shall be sent to the next realm. Be that realm heaven or hell. The Lord has given me the power to release the damned in his mercy to advance them on their way to the next realm. The next passage is to be recited for the release of the damned. Speak the name of the damned, and he shall be set free. He who has sinned has been damned. He who is damned has suffered. He who has suffered has been shown mercy by the light of the Lord. Let that soul advance to the next realm where they shall spend eternity. By the light and mercy of the Lord, we call upon you to release Orrix."

Michael's muscles tightened, waiting for something to happen, but he just watched as Tom and the book fell to the floor. Michael let out a big breath of relief and started to crawl over toward Tom. It was then that he heard a noise from outside the front door. He turned his head to the door, and he could see a figure standing outside the door through the small pane of glass. In his mind, Michael hoped that it was the police or someone else, but he knew exactly who it was. The door opened as fast as a mousetrap slamming shut, and in the doorway stood a tall figure wearing a black shroud. It was Orrix, Michael was certain of it.

Michael began to shake Tom's limp body. "Tom? Can you hear me Tom? Get up. Get up, Tom!"

Tom continued to lay there motionless as Orrix stepped further into the house toward their position. Michael looked up and sat in awe as he finally saw the face of Orrix. Michael had envisioned this figure with a demonic face, unnaturally colored skin, and dark, long hair, but instead, he saw a regular man. Michal noticed Orrix's brown hair, blue eyes, and his medium build. Looking closer, Orrix had the face of an angel. His face was thin and of good complexion as well as handsome. He stared at him in wonderment. His hands were shaking against Tom, and then once again, he felt as if he was frozen. He felt intrigued but frightened at the same time.

Orrix turned his palms up out on front of himself and began to speak, "Am I what you expected, Michael?" Then he placed his hands back down. "Well, what were you expecting, some sort of winged beast? Oh, wait let me guess. A gothic looking man with long hair walking around in all black clothing or perhaps a cape? Well, sorry to disappoint you." His eyes now shifted down toward Tom who lay beside Michael. "As for you, Thomas, you have served your purpose."

"No! I won't let you touch him!" Michael stood up and began to run toward Orrix. He clenched his fists and took a swing at him, but Orrix moved too fast for him and grabbed him by the throat. Michael gagged as he was being lifted off the ground. He felt the air being trapped in his throat, and he couldn't breathe. Orrix pulled Michael close to his face to look him in the eyes.

"Michael, do you think you can really stop me? You are nothing but a weak and pathetic mortal. Just like the rest of your pathetic species. Neither you nor anyone can or will stop me." Orrix focused past Michael where he saw Tom coming to and starting to stand. "Now watch as I rip your friend apart." Orrix threw Michael against the steps. Michael let out a yell of pain as his back thrust against the banister at the end of the steps.

Tom's eyes fixed onto Michael, who now lay facedown on the floor wincing in pain then onto Orrix who was slowly walking toward him. "Who the fu—" Before Tom could finish, Orrix had slashed his throat. Michael sat in horror as the blood began to flow from Tom's neck. It ran down his chest as Tom reached up toward his neck in surprise.

Orrix smiled. "I always loved this part of the kill." Orrix grabbed Tom by his shirt and began to lift him up to his level. He brought Tom close to him and stared into his eyes. "The look of wonderment that is in the eyes, that look of surprise, that look that screams, this can't really be happening. Well, guess what, Thomas? This is happening, and I will tear you limb from limb. Your friend will watch as I bathe in your blood." Orrix began to laugh.

Michael stood up and began to step forward but stopped and fell to the floor and began to vomit as Orrix ripped off one of Tom's arms. It seemed as if he had been ripping a sheet of paper. A muffled sound escaped from Tom's body. He held the torn appendage over his mouth and let the blood drip into his mouth. He smiled with his eyes closed enjoying the moment. He dropped Tom's arm then ripped off the other one. Orrix then laid his twitching body onto the floor and plunged his fist into Tom's abdomen as if he was punching into a pillow. He pushed his arm in further and began to pull. When he pulled his hand free, Tom's heart was sitting in his hand dripping of blood. The blood from Tom's body splashed upon Orrix's face. Then he began to walk over toward Michael. The blood was dripping from Orrix's chin and hand as it came splattering down beside Michael.

"And how are we doing, Michael?"

Michael was on his hands and knees wiping remnants of vomit and saliva from his lips. Then he raised his head to look at Orrix. His voice was muffled from the vomiting he had done. "You bastard. Tom. Tom. You lied to me all along."

Orrix lowered his hand containing the heart and blood splattered onto Michael's face. He cringed at the touch of it on his skin. "Now, Michael, you chose to believe everything I said. Besides, not everything I said were lies. I told you that I needed to return to where I belong, and now I am back where I belong, and, yes, your role in all of this is in fact finally over. Now you can go on living your life in regret and sorrow." Orrix began to laugh.

Michael looked over at Orrix's hand and saw blood dripping off his fingertips. His fingernails weren't of dramatic length. He began to wonder how he had cut Tom's throat. Perhaps it was the exhaustion from being thrown around like a baseball and throwing up or perhaps it was the pure horror of the situation, but Michael passed out. Orrix looked around the room briefly then decided that he had to hide Tom's body. After all, Orrix knew he just couldn't leave a body lying around that would create suspicion and could cause people to start investigating, but if he hid the body, he knew that people wouldn't believe Michael because there was no proof. Orrix began to think of where to hide the body. He looked over at the stairs; he walked up them a bit and noticed the floorboard that had been snapped off. He decided to loosen some boards and put him under the floor. He carried Tom's body and arms up the stairs and got started. After he was done, he looked down at Michael once more then he left.

Michael woke up in shock as if waking up from a bad dream. He looked around with wide eyes as he breathed in and out heavily. He looked for Tom's body, but only saw a throw rug where Tom's body was. What did Orrix do with it? Michael stood up and began to look at the bloodstains on the floor. There was dirt that had been rubbed into the spots of blood. Michael began to look around the room once more then squinted his eyes shut. He had a heavy feeling of fatigue and began to sway front to back then stumbled to the right. Then Michael fell to the floor, tired and broken. Drops of blood stained his forehead as he breathed in and out erratically. Aside from his breath, he lay there motionless for a moment. His eyes lay closed as he let the cool night air pass over and through his exhausted body. He opened his eyes and took in the surrounding room in the old house. It was mostly dark and cold, but the moonbeams seemed to find their way in through the remnants of one of the windows like little beams of cold light, offering true comfort or warmth. His back was on a dust- and dirt-covered floor with broken boards scattered across it. He listened as the entire structure seemed to creak as the chilling wind swept through it like that of a creaking ship blowing in the wind lost at sea.

He pushed his heels into the blood-soaked wood to push his body toward the nearest wall. Exhaling and wincing, he struggled to move. His body felt like someone was standing on his chest as he tried to move. As he neared the wall, he lifted himself up a little and let his back slump against the wall. He raised his shaking hands and cupped his forehead. He looked at the blood on the floor and on himself. He ran his hand through his short, dirty, and blood-spattered black hair then quickly pulled his hand back in frustration. He began to mutter to himself, "Shit…what have I done?" Tears began to form in his brown eyes. "What have I done?" Michael sat there, hands trembling, thinking about what had brought him to this house in the first place.

"You helped to release a demon that I had worked so hard to contain," a voice echoed.

Michael's body twitched as his eyes began to gaze across the room. "What? Who's there?"

"Calm yourself, Michael," the voice added.

Michael's eyes were open wide now. "That voice, I know that voice."

"I was the one who spoke to you in the shower, in the bathroom, and tonight before you came here and released that traitorous demon."

Michael thought for a moment and was scared to say what was in his head. "So, wait, if you are the one who tried to contain him, that means that you're...you're—"

"Go ahead. Say it," the voice said challengingly.

Michael cleared his throat. "That you're the devil."

"Bravo, Michael. A brilliant deduction. Now, let us talk about a more pressing matter at hand. Let me be a little more precise. Orrix."

Michael looked furiously around the rooms. "Where are you?"

"Well I am communicating with you through your thoughts, Michael. You see, Michael, I have no real capability to exist physically in your realm anymore."

"What? I don't understand," Michael said.

"Well, allow me to educate you then, and please, no interruptions. You see long ago, when I was an archangel for God, I fought many battles and did God's bidding, but as time went on, I saw how God favored you humans as opposed to us. After all, we were the angels that he had created to do his bidding and serve his will. He gave you souls and free will while he left us with nothing but a life of slavery. I had decided that this would simply not do, so I started a rebellion in heaven. Many others, as well as myself, decided that God was wrong for choosing you humans over us whom he created first. So, I figured I would just have to defeat God and then I could rule all of the realms as I wished, and we wouldn't be slaves anymore. Thus, a battle began. That battle turned into a war. The heavens had become battlefields where it was angel pitted against angel. Ultimately, as you must already know, I lost that battle, and I was cast down into the furthest depths of what you know as hell. Those who fought with me and survived were cast down with me as well. You must understand that when I was cast down into hell, God made it impossible for me to return to your realm. That is why I have no physical capability here. For centuries, I had tried to find ways to escape, but I could not find a way. It was soon after that I decided that I had lost that battle, but I refused to lose the war."

Michael straightened up and cleared his throat. He his eyes were looking down toward the floor fixed on no particular spot. He was completely concentrated on the voice in his head.

"In my rage, I had seemed to gain powers of creation. Nowhere near the powers of God, but powers nonetheless. It was then I decided to make a being comparable to myself but in no way superior. Someone to go forth into your realm and to do my bidding and to capture the souls that we angels could never have. This is how Orrix came to be. As I am sure, he told you he began working through deceit and corruption, but his powers started to grow, and he became quite good, so I bestowed upon him the power to make his own kind to serve him and ultimately me. These beings where what you had come to know as vampires."

"So, Orrix is just a vampire now?" Michael asked.

"In a way, yes, but understand he is the first and is not immune to many of the weaknesses that his spawn is vulnerable to."

"So, he can't be killed?" Michael asked.

"I didn't say that. In his creation, I had to make a way to be able to destroy him in case he decided to rise up against me as I once did against God. And what I foresaw had started to become a reality. Orrix had served me for many centuries as a loyal servant; however, in the year 1852, I had discovered there had been a rumor of a rebellion in hell. Now, this had been no surprise to me. There had been so many rebellions, but no one was ever able to succeed against me. There many kings, princes, and dukes whose loyalties to me are questionable at best. Well, they were either destroyed or were too weak to stand up in defiance. This latest attempt was treated no differently. I waited for thirty years for some kind of action from the rebellious demons, and it was in the year 1882 that some demons started refusing to do my bidding. So, I dealt with them in reasonable fashion."

"What did you do to them?" Michael asked.

"I destroyed them. After all, I can't have disloyalty and dis-obedience in my realm. Anyway, it was finally in the year 1884 that I had begun to get frustrated at these rumors of rebellion and decided to take drastic action. I began gathering up all of the traitorous demons and tortured them for information. Many were stubborn and many preferred to be destroyed, so I obliged them, others were sent to purgatory to suffer for eternity with no chance of escape. After that, things were fine for a while. The following year it sparked up again. So once more, I began gather-ing up demons. While I was torturing a demon, he had told me that Orrix would reign supreme and that in the end I would be kneeling before him. With him having said that, I sent for Orrix. When I brought him before me and told him of the foul plot at hand, he seemed shocked. I accused him of conspiracy, and he swore that it was not true and repeatedly swore his allegiance, but I knew his powers had been growing ever since I spawned him, and it could very well be just a matter of time before my predic-tion came true. I couldn't risk it, and demons are very untrust-worthy by nature, and after all, he was made from me, the lord of lies. Still, I couldn't find it in me to destroy him, so I decided to banish him to the realm of waiting, purgatory. I see now that was a mistake."

Michael interjected, "Orrix had told me that was how he ended up there."

"Please, Michael, there is more. I had banished him to purgatory for eternity. It was not until recently that I had discovered his plot. After all, I am not all-knowing, God never made me that powerful."

"So, his plot was to return to the mortal realm?"

"That's only part of it, Michael. He has not only been plotting to return to the mortal realm but to make his kind live once again and ultimately get revenge for me not believing him and sending him to purgatory. He plans to conquer hell so he can rule supreme and do to me what I did to him."

"Well, why don't you just summon him back and banish him again?"

"He has grown far too powerful for me to just summon him. He will simply disregard my summoning. That is why I need your help."

Michael's head shot up in surprise. "My help! Why in God's name would you want my help?" Michael's voice broke off as he began to feel a pain in his head and tightness in his chest. He leaned forward as he clenched at his chest.

"God has nothing to do with this. I am sure God is just sitting up high, laughing at the mess I have created. God probably can't wait for me to lose dominion over hell. Oh, and to answer your question of why. You were the one who led the Matheson descendant to this place. It was you who allowed Orrix to escape, and it is you who are going to help fix this situation."

Michael was letting out whimpers from the pain in his head. The tightness in his chest made it difficult for him to speak. "And if I refuse?"

"If you refuse…" The pain began to increase in Michael's head, and blood started to run from his nose. "If you refuse, I will kill you right now."

Michael wiped the blood from his face. "Go ahead, I'd rather die!" Michael's breaths were heavy and full of anger and pain.

"You know that's not true, Michael. Look deep into your mind and tell me as I push you closer to the brink of death that you really wish to die!"

Michael began to turn pale as his air supply was being cut off. Blood was coming out of both nostrils, and his body began to convulse rapidly. His eyes rolled back into his head, and he was now lying on his back as the blood ran down his throat and tears ran from his eyes. "Now, Michael, tell me, do you still want to die?" Lucifer asked.

The blood in his throat made it difficult for him to talk. He coughed up a few times then began to answer, "N-n-no…"

Lucifer released his grip on him. Michael took in a great breath and started to breathe faster and faster. After a few seconds, he began to slow his breathing but took in more air with every one of his breaths. He sat up and coughed up a large wad of blood and mucus. He spat it out onto the floor as tears continued to run from his eyes. He began to whisper to himself, "Why is this happening? God, please help me."

"God cannot help you now, Michael. Look at it this way, you can confront Orrix and try to destroy him or you can die now, and we both know you don't want to die."

The words began to creep from his lips wrapped in sadness. "No… I don't." He tried to raise his arms to wipe his tears, but he had no energy in his body.

"Rest now, Michael, and when you awaken, we will discuss what to do about Orrix."

"Aren't you worried about him coming for you?"

"We have little time, this is true, but I know where he is going, and when he arrives, you and I will be there waiting for him. So, rest now, Michael. We will speak again when you awaken." Michael slowly shut his eyes and fell asleep.

When Michael opened his eyes, he was lying on his back. He could feel the trails of blood on his throat and on his face. It was very uncomfortable, so he decided to find something to wipe away the blood. He tried to stand and fell back to the floor. He gritted his teeth as sounds of pain and frustration escaped between them. He closed his eyes and took a deep breath. He placed his hands on the banister of the steps and began to raise himself up. He looked up the stairs and saw a bathroom in the hallway at the top of the steps. He sighed in disappointment and began to ascend up the steps. He could feel the majority of his weight resting in his arms.

He made it to the top of the steps and placed his left hand against the wall and began to move slowly down the hallway. He walked into the bathroom and saw mildew around the sink and bathtub. He walked over to the toilet and raised the lid. The water level was low and was stagnant. The smell was that of a mixture of feces and urine mixed with the stagnant water. He knew the lights wouldn't work, but he decided to try the sink. Nothing. He moved over toward the bathtub and turned the tarnished silver handles. Again nothing. He looked over at the toilet and at the water inside. The thought crossed his mind only once, but the smell made him decide against it. Then he remembered there was water in the tank of the toilet. He removed the cover from the tank. The water level was low and stagnant like the rest of the toilet.

"At least this water doesn't have shit and piss in it," Michael said.

Michael reached down and cupped a handful of water and began to wipe the blood from his throat and face. He cringed at the smell of the water and came close to vomiting from it. Even though it had smelled awful, it felt good on his skin. He enjoyed the feeling of the water running down his throat to his chest. For a moment, the smell disappeared, and he lost himself in the sensation. He felt very relaxed. He shook the excess water from his hand and placed the cover back on the toilet's tank. For a moment, he thought why he had even bothered to put it back on. It wasn't like anyone would complain. He searched around for a towel or a piece of cloth to dry himself with. After finding nothing in the bathroom, he dried his hands on his pant legs then he removed his hooded sweatshirt and tried to find a clean spot to wipe the water from his face.

Michael walked back downstairs and looked around the room and became short of breath thinking about what had happened. He didn't want to be in this house any longer, so he walked outside and stopped on the porch. He began debating about driving back to his apartment. He was feeling very nervous and disturbed, so he got back in Tom's car. He knew he would need to return the car, but without Tom's phone, he didn't know where to bring it let alone when it needed to be back. He realized nothing could be done about it, so he prepared to go home.

"Keys…where are the keys?" Instinctively, he looked around the car then it hit him. "Tom…"

Michael remembered that the keys were in Tom's possession. Michael sat in the car for a moment, contemplating about finding his remains and getting the keys from them, but he started to feel nauseous thinking about what had happened. He thought about using his phone to get a ride, but he knew that if anyone saw him looking the way that he did, they would probably ask questions, plus he didn't want to risk anyone seeing any part of what happened here tonight, so he decided he would just walk home. He exited the car, shut the door, and stood once more, staring at the house, but this time, he stood alone. He sighed, then turned and began walking back toward the main road. He removed his phone from his pocket and opened his maps app and got walking directions back to his apartment. The app said that it would take him three hours and twenty-seven minutes to walk the eight miles back to his apartment. He put his phone away, zipped up his hoodie, and kept walking.

While he was walking home, he had noticed how beautiful the moon had looked and how the glow from it seemed to comfort him. He was sitting on the side of Route 34 taking a break. It was very late and there were practically no cars out. According to his phone, he had about an hour until he reached campus then another fifteen minutes till he made it to his apartment. He stood up, stretched his arms and started out once again.

Michael began thinking of all kinds of things on his way home. They had no real order as they just popped up in his mind. Tom, Orrix, Lucifer, the book, God, and, of course, Olivia. He missed her deeply. He thought about how short of a time he knew Olivia and began to wonder if his feelings were genuine.

Was it the fact that she died and he felt responsible? Perhaps he felt he owed it to her to follow through with this task now at hand and that if he didn't, she would have died for nothing. Tom too. He was starting to doubt his feelings when he shook his head to try to clear his mind. He knew that deep down, his feelings were genuine and that he cared for Olivia. His thoughts moved toward Tom. They had been friends since freshman year. How would Michael tell his family about what had happened? What could he really say? Michael let out a sigh. His was full of confusion. There was so much that had happened and so much more left to be done.

Michael had been walking for about forty-five minutes when he sat down again for a moment on the side of the road. He was getting thirsty now. He was kicking at the grass as he kept thinking about Tom.

"That fucking asshole. Orrix, you asshole! I'll make you pay."

After a few minutes, Michael stood up and continued to walk toward campus. Clouds were starting to move over the moon. He watched as the nimbus clouds passed over the glow of the moon, and he couldn't help but think how beautiful it all seemed. Michael was walking down the sidewalk through the university now. He looked around at the trees and how they were moving in the wind. He stopped and stared at them. The movement of the trees seemed to relax him. It made him think of how a mother rocked her baby to sleep. He closed his eyes and felt the cool wind pass over his face. He was starting to feel exhausted again and knew that he had to get home before he passed out on the lawn. He opened his eyes and made his way to his apartment.

He walked into the building, continued over toward the elevator and pressed the call button. He waited for the doors to open then stepped inside. Pretty soon, he would be able to sit down in a chair and relax. His whole body seemed to ache. He couldn't wait to take a shower to cleanse himself. He kept thinking if the shower would cleanse him of what had happened tonight. He looked at his watch, 3:47 a.m., and then the elevator doors opened. He walked down the hallway to his apartment. He opened the door and walked inside. Once inside, he was hit with a wave of fatigue. It was almost as if his body knew it had reached a safe place and could finally relax. He shut the door then walked over toward the couch. He flopped down and started to think again about everything that had happened at the house. He squeezed his eyes shut tight at the vision of Tom in his mind in an effort to shut it all out. He wanted to get back up and go shower, but his body protested, and he continued to sit on the couch. With his mind racing like it was now, he worried that he wouldn't be able to sleep. He saw the television remote on the table. He reached for it then turned on the TV. It was some infomercial about a tabletop roasting machine. He was asleep in three minutes.

CHAPTER 12

Monday, April 30

Michael awoke to the sound of some soap opera on the TV. In annoyance, he reached forward for the remote and turned off the TV. Michael wasn't about to start thinking that everything that had happened last night was just a dream. He knew it had happened, and while he didn't know what would come next, he knew that he was inescapably tied to it. He stood up and made his way toward the bathroom. He stopped in his bedroom and had a moment of reflection. He stared at his bed with a look of hatred. *This is where it all started*, he kept thinking. He looked away and continued into the bathroom. He looked down at his clothes in disgust as he began to peel them off his body. He turned the showerhead on and waited for the water to become warm. Michael never could take hot showers.

Fifteen minutes later, Michael came out of the bathroom, walked over to his dresser, and pulled out some clothes to change into. After getting dressed, he put on his socks and then he stood up to go get his boots from the other room. That was when he heard Lucifer's voice.

"Ready for another day, Michael?" he said.

Michael stopped walking and straightened up. "I was waiting for you to come," Michael said.

"I'm flattered, Michael," the sarcasm was blatant in Lucifer's
response.

"I'm surprised you didn't do it in the shower again," Michael
said.

"That wouldn't be right to torture you now, especially after
you have agreed to cooperate."

Michael smirked. "How kind of you. So, before we go any
further, something has been bothering me, and I would like to ask
about it."

There was a pause before Lucifer replied, "Fine. What is it?"

"Now I am just going off stories and I guess movies here,
but supposedly all throughout history, there have been stories of
people making all sorts of deals with you and seeing you. What I
was wondering is if you can't physically come to earth, how did
those things happen?"

"Well, truth be told, most of these stories people have heard
are hoaxes. Now there have been deals made sure, I love a deal,
but they were perpetrated by my minions, many by Orrix himself. They were acting in my place or on my instruction."

"So, in the case of Orrix, he was turning these people into
vampires for you?"

"At my instruction, yes. No more questions now. It's time
to go."

"Where?" Michael inquired.

"To get a newspaper. Time to see if Orrix has begun turning
others."

"But wait a minute, if all this happened last night, how in
the world are the newspapers gonna write a story?"

"Michael, it's Monday. You slept through yesterday."

Michael was confused for only a second, but he thought about it, and then he knew that it was possible. He was so intensely exhausted that he wasn't surprised. Michael grabbed his phone. "Why don't I just look it up on my phone?"

"Ah, youth and your phones. The newspapers will be faster, besides, do you even know all the local papers? I doubt it. Stop at that shop you like to go to and get a bunch of them. Anyone that has gone missing will be listed in the local papers. He couldn't have gotten terribly far in just two days, but we need to check all the local papers to be certain."

Michael nodded and put his phone away. He grabbed his keys and wallet then headed out the door toward the cafeteria. On his way, he stopped at a convenience store and bought three separate local papers. The cover story on one of them was about some political figure involved in some scandal. Michael scoffed. "Now there's a surprise." Michael continued on toward the cafeteria. He went inside to get himself a drink and a bite to eat. He walked in and felt a sudden sense of paranoia. He started looking at people strangely and wondered if Orrix was near. After all, he could be around in the daytime since he wasn't vulnerable to the things that could hurt his spawn. Michael looked quizzically at a boy in a red hoodie that had stared at Michael for only a second. Michael brushed the feeling off. He thought about how people look at strangers all the time when someone crosses their gaze and that it was probably nothing.

He walked over to the drink refrigerators and grabbed a bottle of iced tea. After that, he went and looked at the bagels, but the thought of eating made him sick. He started to get visions of what had happened to Tom and quickly decided against getting something to eat. He paid for his drink and then walked over to an empty table to sit down. He muttered to himself, "Good thing finals don't start till tomorrow." He started to think about how it hardly seemed important now, but he pushed those thoughts away. He had to believe that there was a future after this, that life could go on. Anytime his mind started to drift to a feeling of hopelessness, he pulled himself back. He had to do whatever he could to hang on to that hope. Michael began to open the first newspaper when a story on the bottom caught his eye. Five college students had been reported missing on their way back from a party. There was no sign of the car or the students. Witnesses were quoted in saying that the students left the party around 3:00 a.m. He opened the next paper and under local crimes, he saw a story about a domestic dispute where the man accused was suspected to have kidnapped the woman involved. The neighbors were quoted in reporting screaming and the sounds of fighting or a struggle. One neighbor went over when the screaming had stopped and said that there was blood everywhere. The third paper showed no stories of interest.

"That's it, Michael." Michael heard Lucifer say. He didn't answer right away as he was afraid of what everyone in the cafeteria would think seeing him talking to himself. "It's okay, Michael, I can read your thoughts."

Michael started speaking to himself in his mind, "Wait, you can read my thoughts?"

"Yes, Michael. I am the devil. That does afford one some interesting powers."

Annoyed, Michael closed his eyes and bit his lower lip. "Can you please stop calling me Michael? Between you and Orrix, it's driving me nuts! Michael this and Michael that. Please, just Mike will do. Aside from you, guys, only my grandmother called me Michael, and she's dead."

Lucifer snapped, "I'll call you whatever I want!"

Michael closed his eyes and pursed his lips, immediately regretting that he had asked. "I was just trying to s—"

Lucifer interjected, "Now listen up, *Michael!* Those stories you read are Orrix's doing. I am certain of it."

"What, the college students? The domestic dispute?" Michael asked.

"Yes. Missing with no evidence, no witnesses."

"Yeah, so what? They probably just kept driving after the party to go on a road trip. I mean it's not unheard of. My friends and I did it one semester ourselves. And the domestic thing, I've seen documentaries about that kind of stuff. It happens more than people realize."

Lucifer replied, "Come now, that one is more obvious. The screaming, the struggle, the blood." Michael nodded in agreement. "It's his doing. Everything is happening just as I knew it would."

"So, you predicted this to happen? The disappearance?" Michael involuntarily chuckled while he reached for his iced tea. He began to feel the cool beverage enter his mouth and splash against his tongue when his throat felt as if it had shut and nothing could pass through it. It was then that he spit out the iced tea across the table. People looked over toward him in surprise. Embarrassed, Michael wiped his face and looked at those around him. "Sorry. I'm all right," he said as he looked around some more and noticed some people laughing. He shook his head in annoyance then wiped his face with his sleeve as he had no napkins. He stood up to go get some napkins to wipe the table down.

"Do you know why I did that, *Mike*?"

Michael sighed. "Yeah, I'm sorry. I just thought that—"

"Be sure it doesn't happen again."

Michael returned to the table, sat down and started wiping up the mess he had made. "Okay, so Orrix is responsible. That means what exactly?"

"Don't you remember what I told you that night in the church?"

"Honestly, I've been trying to forget that whole night," Michael said.

"Orrix is starting to spawn more of his kind in an attempt to lead an assault on hell."

"Well, don't you have like a million demons or something like that?" Michael asked.

"I have kings, princes, dukes, and marquises of hell who command many legions. The problem here is that I need to do this myself. I cannot risk having the rest of my flock seeing a possible rebellion. I need to keep this contained and use only my closest, most loyal followers. As most demons are deceitful and untrustworthy to start, I need to be extra careful in who I have help me with his. Because of that, I won't have that many people there when Orrix comes. Plus, his demons will be formidable as is Orrix, and he knows all of this. But that's okay because I know something Orrix doesn't."

"And what's that?" Michael asked.

"That, as you might say, is for me to know and you to find out. Now, Michael, I need you to tell me how this all started. I need to know why he came to you. I need to understand this more to ensure I am not missing something."

Michael proceeded to tell of all the events that led up to the present moment. He spoke of the dreams, of Olivia, Tom, the visions of purgatory, as well as the story of Matheson. Of how Orrix had tortured him and threatened him to do his bidding over the course of the past month. Of how Orrix had lied to him. That he had wanted Tom all along and how he was simply a way to get to Tom, a pawn. Michael became flooded with emotion while rehashing all these events. A tear began to form in the corner of his eye. It rolled down across his cheek and to his chin. It fell and splashed down onto the newspaper like a drop of rain falling to the earth. The moisture immediately affecting the newspaper and its ink. He wiped his face and continued on about the things that Orrix had spoken of, about returning to where he belonged, and how he seemed to have felt cheated.

Lucifer began to speak. "I can see how he feels cheated. I know he was innocent, but in time, he would try to conquer hell, I'm certain of it, and I cannot have that happen. Hell belongs to me and no one else. Not even God has a say of what happens there. And I'll be damned if some demon takes control of what is mine!" Lucifer could sense something was stirring in Michael. "What is it, Michael?"

Michael shook his head. "Nothing."

"There's confusion in your mind. You're trying to figure out where all this is headed. Well just remember this, Orrix is a demon created by my hand, nothing more. He will tremble at my feet when I am through with him. I created him, and I can destroy him."

"So, now what do we do?" Michael asked.

"Now you go home. I will contact you later."

Michael sat at the table for a moment and reflected on what he was told about how Lucifer knew something that Orrix didn't. It didn't surprise him, but his natural curiosity wanted so badly to know what it was. Michael stood up and made his way out of the cafeteria. He finished his iced tea and threw the bottle along with the newspapers in the recycle bin then made his way to the door. He stepped outside and paused as he felt the warmth of the sunshine upon his face. He raised his head and closed his eyes at the brightness. The light began to feel hot on his skin, but at the same time, he found it relaxing. He stood there for a moment as a breeze passed over his body. He took a deep breath and opened his eyes as he exhaled then continued onward. It occurred to him that he seemed to be finding more beauty in the world around him recently. He remembered how he was at a standstill at one point on the night he was walking home from the old house. How two days ago he lay in bed in awe when he awoke to the beauty of the day. Perhaps it was the combination of the recent events that made him understand how important everything was. Or maybe it was something else. He tried not to dwell on it too long. He began to walk up the sidewalk when a man in a suit and tie approached him. He had a book in one hand and what appeared to be pamphlets in the other. It was then the man spoke.

"Excuse me, son?"

"Yes?" Michael asked.

"Have you ever given any thought to the kingdom of heaven?"

Michael scoffed. "Heaven can't help us now. Please go away."

The man stared at him in awe and confusion. He back-pedaled for a few steps then turned and walked away. Michael watched as he left and then turned back once again to look at Michael before continuing away. Shortly after, Michael walked inside his apartment building and walked over to the mailboxes to get his mail. As he was opening his mailbox, he heard footsteps behind him followed by a familiar voice.

"Excuse me?"

"Yes, can I help—" Michael broke off as he was staring again at the man in the suit and tie holding the book. "Look, I already told you that I am not interested in the kingdom of heaven. So just leave me—"

The man interrupted, "Alone. I understand. But understand this, Michael."

Michael stood in total surprise. "How do you—"

"I read it on one of your letters. Forgive me for intruding." Michael sighed in relief. "I was just wondering if you ever questioned your faith?"

Michael's shoulders dropped in annoyance. "Look, I don't really have time to talk about this with you right now." Michael stared close at the man's face. "Hey, haven't we met before?"

The man shook his head. "No, I don't think so, but if you are in need of someone to talk to or need guidance in any way, feel free to stop by."

The man handed Michael a pamphlet from inside his suit jacket. Michael took it from his hand and replied. "Thanks… I'll think about it."

"Have a wonderful day, sir." The man nodded his head and began to walk away.

Michael stood there for a moment then looked down at the pamphlet and then grabbed the rest of his mail. He made his way into the elevator, and just as the doors shut, he dropped his mail and winced in pain as he felt his head begin to throb, and a sharp ringing sound echoed through his ears. Then Lucifer's voice came through.

"You fool! Do you have any idea who you were just talking to?" Michael couldn't answer due to the pain in his head. "Orrix, you stupid son of a bitch! Didn't you recognize him?" Lucifer asked.

Michael opened his eyes and mouth wide in an attempt to loosen his face and jaw and relieve the pain inside. "I thought… he looked familiar. But something in my mind told me it wasn't him."

"Humans, so easy to control. Don't you see? He manipulated you. What did he give you?"

"Some pamphlet. It's in the pile here somewhere." Michael began to brush away letters and magazines as he looked for the pamphlet. He found it after a few seconds. He picked it up and began to stand as he turned it over. There was writing on the back of it. It read, "I know what you are trying to do, and I will be ready for you."

Lucifer's voice echoed through Michael's mind in furious anger. "That hapless imp! Disastrous fortune awaits you, my rebellious solider. Your time is at an end, I assure you. As long as the fires in hell continue to burn, I will not falter. Time is growing short, Michael. I will return to you tomorrow, for now I must go make preparations for Orrix's arrival. Until that time, make no action or mention of what is going on and tell no one of what has happened because if you do, the price will be dear, I assure you. Do you understand?"

Michael stood with his eyes fixated on the floor. He thought about how he didn't really have anyone he could tell anyway.

Everyone he told so far was dead. He uttered the words out of his lips, "Yes, I understand." Michael looked up as the elevator doors opened. He was still on the main floor. There was a couple standing there in the hall just outside of the elevator doors, and they just stared at him as he stood there with his mail lying at his feet. Michael tried to play off the situation and reached down to scoop up the mail. As he stood up, he realized that he was standing in front of the elevator's buttons. "Oh, sorry. Uh, what floor?" he asked as the couple walked in.

The first girl replied, "Uh, fourth floor, thanks."

Michael pushed the button labeled 3 and then the one labeled 4. His breathing was staggered as the elevator doors closed.

Back in his apartment, Michael was sitting in his kitchen staring into his glass of soda. He stared as the bubbles formed at the bottom and made their way up to the surface. They reminded him of the balloons he used to set free when he was young. How he would stand and stare as they rose toward the sky higher and higher until they couldn't even be seen anymore. The radio was on in the background. He blinked his eyes as if wiping clean the thoughts in his mind. They now shifted toward his finals. Michael knew the unspoken rule about not having to take three finals on one day, but it never bothered him. He always felt he worked his best under pressure. Besides after Thursday, he wouldn't have to worry about them. He could relax, but he knew that Satan was going to come for his help tomorrow. Part of him began to think of the possible inconvenience if Lucifer were to come during one of his finals, what would he do then? There was a part of him that saw no point in even going to take the finals, but he just wanted some normalcy, and even a college final was good enough for him. Michael placed his cup onto the table and then placed his hands on either side of his head. He ran his fingers through his hair as he exhaled fiercely, almost as if he were trying to blow out a birthday candle. He rubbed his forehead and then his eyes. Tilting his head backward, he extended his arms into the air to stretch and began to yawn while arching his back. He felt a crack give way in his back, which felt good.

Michael stood up and walked over to get the mail that he had placed on the coffee table. He picked up that pamphlet which he had received from that man, who according to Lucifer was Orrix deceiving him somehow. Lucifer insisted that it was him, so it must have been him, but Michael knew deep down that he couldn't be trusted. After all, he's the devil. He crumpled the pamphlet in his hands and threw into the trash. He looked at the rest of the mail, and there were letters from some technical school, a credit card company, a little postcard about the local newspaper delivery, and a newspaper with some coupons. For a moment, he wondered why he even went to pick up his mail anymore. He pushed that thought aside and sat back down. He started to think about purgatory.

Orrix referred to it as a place of waiting. Which meant that if demons were taking souls away, why weren't angels doing the same? Why weren't angels helping people? He started to wonder if God even cared about those people, but then he remembered the visions he saw. Those people had all been suffering and were tormented. Perhaps there were other levels of purgatory that he just hadn't seen or wasn't made to see. Perhaps Orrix only wanted him to see those places so that perhaps he would feel more compelled to help him leave. Then he thought that maybe none of it was real and Orrix just made him see those visions to slowly break him down and unnerve him. Michael sighed. He wasn't really sure what to believe anymore. He began to wonder why he was even going through with this whole thing or if he even had the strength to follow through with it. Michael hadn't considered himself a very religious person. Sure, he believed in God, but he had never really gone to church past the time his parents had him get his communion. He didn't pray, generally, but he found himself questioning his faith, questioning God. He wondered if God really did care about what was actually happening to him, to Lucifer, and the consequences that could very well affect all of hell.

The day continued to drag on for Michael. He thought about going out for a walk, but he was scared he might run into Orrix again. He started to think how he didn't even recognize him. After the ordeal he went through, he wondered how he could forget his face. Perhaps it wasn't Orrix at all, perhaps it was a trick being pulled by Lucifer to make Michael cooperate, to make him uneasy so he could be manipulated like Orrix had done. He wasn't really sure, but his thoughts shifted to the possibility of Lucifer or Orrix reading his thoughts right then and there. Then he remembered how Lucifer himself had even said that he was not all-knowing and that only God was. Michael drew the conclusion that Orrix was not as well since he was spawned from Lucifer. Michael stood up and began to pace back and forth across his apartment. He needed to use the bathroom, so he headed in and shut the door, undid his pants, and slid them down with his underwear then sat on the toilet. After he finished, he pulled his clothes back up, flushed, and then washed his hands. He stared at himself in the mirror for a moment then let out a sigh.

He exited the bathroom and headed into the kitchen. Michael stopped suddenly as a man was bent over looking in the refrigerator. Michael froze with fear and looked around quickly for something to defend himself with. He could only find a large textbook, so he picked it up and held it up over his shoulder like a baseball bat ready to swing. It was then that the man spoke.

"Hey, Mike, don't you have any iced tea?"

Michael froze and felt confused. "I know that voice," he said.

"You bet you do, Mikey."

Michael froze for a moment. "T-Tom?"

The man stood up and faced Michael. "What's up?"

Michael was shaking his head in utter disbelief. "That can't be you. It can't be."

"Don't you have any iced tea, dude?"

Tears began to fill Michael's eyes as he walked toward Tom, dropping the textbook on the floor. He couldn't believe what he was seeing.

"Mike, are you all right?"

Michael leaped forward and hugged Tom. "I thought you were dead. I saw you die. I watched..." Michael struggled to finish the sentence as the visions of what had happened to Tom flooded his mind. "I watched you get ripped apart."

"That's right you did, and what did you do to try and help me?"

Michael took a step back as tears were rolling down his face. "Tom... I mean, I...what could I do?" Michael shrugged his arms and shoulders. "I tried to stop him, but he was just too strong." Tom just stared blankly at Michael. "I'm sorry. I should have tried harder. I'm so sorry, Tom. Please, forgive me."

"Forgive you?" Tom turned away from Michael and faced the open refrigerator door. "I should be thanking you, Michael."

Michael felt his sadness subside quickly as the voice he heard now was not Tom's anymore. It was Orrix, Michael knew that for certain. Orrix was still facing away from him when he continued speaking, "I should be thanking you for setting me free, for bringing me Tom." Orrix turned around, and he no longer looked like Tom. He looked as Michael recalled from the night at the old house. Orrix continued, "And for the pleasure that I had ripping him apart and tasting his blood."

Michael backed away quickly as he tried to catch his breath and speak at the same time. He stumbled as he walked backward and almost fell doing so. Orrix began walking toward Michael.

"Michael, calm down." Orrix laughed. "I'm only here to kill you."

Michael continued to backpedal away. "No! No! You get away from me! Stay away!" Michael put his hands out in front of him, trying to signal to Orrix to stay away.

Orrix stopped and just stood there as he began to laugh again. Then just as soon as Michael regained his balance, Orrix had vanished. Michael felt his heart skip a beat and then felt it pounding as if trying to escape out of his chest. Michael looked around in astonishment at the now empty space in front of him. He slowly creeped back toward the kitchen looking around furniture, expecting Orrix to pop out from under something like the couch or the coffee table. He saw nothing, so he continued to the kitchen slowly. Again, there was nothing, so he sat down at the table.

Was that really Orrix just now? he thought. *Maybe I am just over tired, I'm just seeing things is all.* He sat there for a moment and thought that he should eat, but the thought of eating something made him feel sick again. He closed his eyes as he felt an acidic taste form in his throat. In his mind, he saw blood, Tom's blood pouring out of his torso where his arms used to be. Michael snapped to and stood up. He shook his head as if trying to shake the thoughts free from his mind. He took a quick drink from his soda, but something tasted off. He ran over to the sink to spit it out, and when he did, there was that taste again, blood. He couldn't believe what he was seeing. He wiped his mouth, and sure enough, it was blood. He spit again in the sink. "What in the hell?" Michael said.

"Is he not to your taste, Michael? I thought he tasted divine," Orrix said, followed by immense laughter.

Michael spun around, wiping his face looking for Orrix, but he saw nothing. He quickly turned back to the sink, and the blood was gone.

Orrix's voice started again, "Oh, I am going to enjoy this. By the time I am done with you, you will be begging me for death." Again, he laughed.

"Just do it already then!" Michael yelled.

Orrix just laughed again. "Oh, Michael. Not on your terms, not a chance. Your time is coming, but I am enjoying feeding off your misery. Tell me what went through your mind while you watched me rip your friend apart? I wasn't really paying attention as I was too busy drinking his blood. Did you even look for him when you woke? Or did you just run away? Some friend you turned out to be."

"Screw you! I hate you!" Michael started hitting his fists against the sides of his head. "Get the fuck out of my head! Get out!" Michael stood defiantly.

"Soon enough, Michael. One day soon, I will come and give you the release you so desire, but not yet. I have matters to attend to, and you'd be wise to keep them to yourself or the release I spoke of will be long and agonizing. Until next time. Good luck on your finals." Orrix started to laugh, and it faded to silence.

Michael walked slowly back to the living room waiting for something else to happen, but it didn't. As his heart started to slow, he took deep breaths and started to fight back more tears. He was filling with rage and at the same time fear. His anger crept out in whispers between sobs. "Fuck. What the fuck!" He crouched down in front of the couch and broke down. "Fucking stop it already! Leave me alone!" He clenched his fists so hard he thought his fingers might break. "I'm sorry! I'm sorry! I'm so sorry, Tom" He lay down on the couch cushions, and in a sub-conscious effort to soothe himself, he pulled his knees up to his chest and lay in a fetal position. He lay there crying uncontrollably. The weight of everything that had happened up until now was as heavy as an anvil now. He felt it crushing him, breaking him, and a part of him just wanted to surrender to everything and just be done with it all in whatever way that meant. Then Michael's phone rang. He opened his eyes and loosened his position then pulled the phone from his pocket. It was his mom. He had been fighting an urge to call her these past few days and ask for help explaining everything that had happened, but he knew that she wouldn't believe him or that in telling her, something would happen to her and his father. He contemplated sending her to voice mail, but decided that in his current state, he really wanted to just hear her voice. He sat up, wiped his face, and took a few deep breaths. He tapped the answer button on his phone and held the phone to his head then started.

"Hey, Mom," he said.

"Hi, sweetheart!" His mom sounded excited to hear his voice. "Oh, I hope I'm not bothering you, but I knew you had finals tomorrow, and I just wanted to call and say good luck. Your father and I both know that you're going to do great."

Michael couldn't help but smile, but it was fleeting as the pressure and stress of everything upon him pushed it down. He wanted to just scream, to cry, to tell his mom everything, but he didn't. "Thanks, Mom." His voice sounded strained. He squeezed his lips together in an effort to hold back all the emotion that was lurking just below the surface.

"Mike, honey, are you all right? You sound a little down. Is there something you want to talk about?" *She always knew*, he thought.

"No, I'm fine, Mom," he said. "It's just... I just...um, I'm really tired from, uh, from studying so much, and, uh, I just worry that maybe I am not as focused as I could be, you know? After all, everything has been building up to tomorrow." *If she only knew*, he thought.

"Oh, sweetheart. It's going to be okay. Just make sure you get some rest tonight and be sure to study if you feel like you aren't totally ready." She caught herself. "I'm sorry. You've been there for four years, and you don't need your mom telling you how to prep for finals, I'm sure." She giggled, and Michael felt a grin form on his face.

"I know, Mom. It's okay, I'll be okay." He questioned that phrase the moment after it left it his lips.

"Well, okay, sweetheart, your father and I are so proud of you. After this week, you'll be all done, and then you'll be able to start the next chapter of your life. I know you'll do great. You just hang in there, okay?"

"I will, Mom, thanks."

"And you know you can call us every once in a while. We know you're busy enjoying college, but we still like to hear from you and not just see pictures on social media."

"I'm sorry, Mom. I have just been…" Michael took a breath. "I have just been busy getting ready for finals is all."

"I know, sweetie, I understand. I just want you to know we're here for you is all."

Michael clenched his lips together and paused before responding, "I know."

"Well, good luck again tomorrow, sweetheart, and tell that Tom we said hello, okay?"

Michael felt his stomach drop. "Uh-huh, okay, look, Mom, I gotta go okay. I uh…" Michael felt the sadness building in him again, so he breathed again to try and stop it from building. "I have to eat something, and then I am going to study before I go to sleep, so I am gonna go, okay?"

"Okay, sweetheart. Knock 'em dead tomorrow. Love you."

Michael hung his head. "I love you too, Mom."

"Okay, bye."

"Bye." Michael tapped the end call button on his phone then held the phone to his forehead as he played back his mom's word over in his head. The pessimistic voice in his head kept repeating the same question in his head over and over again, *What's the point?* He blocked it out and decided that he was going to go to his finals tomorrow. He reaffirmed himself that he needed this.

He needed something to anchor him, or he would drift away and get lost in all this sorrow. He sat up and took some more deep breaths as he tried to steel himself. He stood up and stared at the kitchen. He nibbled on his lower lip and then started to slowly walk back into the kitchen. He felt his breathing stagger as a part of him waited for Orrix to show himself again, but nothing happened. He felt his shoulders relax a bit, and he decided to sit down and try to study. He grabbed a soda from the refrigerator and placed on the table. He returned to the other room to grab his books then went back to the table. He sat down and opened his books, and at first, he just stared at them and felt his focus shift as they went blurry. He caught himself and took a big sip of his soda and reminded himself that he needed this. Needed to feel some normalcy or he would be lost. He grabbed his phone and put on his studying playlist, which consisted of some mellow music, so he could focus. He started to study, and after several hours of reviewing the material for his first final tomorrow, he decided it was time to stop.

He stood up and made his way to get ready for bed. Shortly after that, he was lying in his bed. He was struggling to get to sleep as his mind was racing. After tossing and turning and try-ing to find a comfortable position for about an hour, he finally fell asleep. It was three in the morning when he woke suddenly. His breathing was heavy and staggered. He was trying to recall what had woken him up, but he couldn't place it. He knew that he hadn't been dreaming, or at least he thought he hadn't been. If he had, he could not recall it, and he didn't have any of the normal feelings after the dreams with Orrix. He felt uneasy and grabbed his phone off the bedside. He turned on the flashlight in his phone and used it to pan the room. He saw nothing, turned off the light and returned his phone to the bedside table. He lay back down and stared at the ceiling for a while. Then he rolled to his side, positioned his right hand under his pillow and shut his eyes to try and return to sleep.

CHAPTER 13

Tuesday, May 1

Michael awoke and looked over at his alarm clock, it was 6:38 a.m. He had woken up six more times in the course of the evening, and every time, he looked at the clock in a panic, almost like he had missed an alarm even though none had been set. He began to fidget his toes a bit under the sheets. Sometimes, when he couldn't sleep, simply wiggling his toes helped him fall back asleep. It wasn't working this morning, so he decided that he was done trying to sleep despite the fact that he was still tired. He started to sit up, but his body resisted as his muscles felt tense. He swung his legs over the edge of the bed and just sat there with his eyes closed for a few moments. He truly wanted to go back to sleep, but his mind was racing and he just couldn't. He opened his eyes. The room was dimly lit as the morning sun was breaking on the horizon in the east. Most mornings, he loved that his apartment faced east, but this was not one of them. Annoyed, he stared at the morning sun as it was beginning to creep in through the window. Its orange glow seemed to crawl across the floor as the minutes went by. Michael stood up, stretched his arms into the air, and took a deep breath. He stopped at his dresser, grabbed a change of clothes, and made his way into the bathroom. He stood in front of the toilet to pee and afterward washed his hands then got the shower ready. Once the water was warm enough, he climbed in.

While in the shower, he was running through the material for his first final in his head and then started wondering when he would hear from Lucifer today. He pushed it to the back of his mind as much as he could so he could try to focus. He continually reminded himself that all this was soon to be behind him. A story he planned never to tell anyone. Then he started thinking of Tom. How would he handle the questions when he didn't turn up? What would he do? What would he say? He pushed that away as well and exited the shower. Michael was dressed and out of the door by 8:37 a.m. He arrived at the hall for his class at 8:58 a.m. He was grateful that project management was at the hall right down the road from his place. Other days, Michael took buses to get to other parts of the campus. Michael walked into the classroom and sat down. The professor gave a brief lecture then handed out the exams. Michael stared at the exam in front of him. Inside his mind, he was praying that Lucifer would not come. He took a deep breath and began the exam.

At 10:48 a.m., Michael emerged from his classroom. He let out a great sigh of relief and decided that he would go to the coffee shop down the road between here and his apartment. His next final wasn't until twelve o'clock, so he had time to go get a nice cup of coffee. The weather was nice and cool, so he decided to walk to the coffee shop. He entered the coffee shop, and the line wasn't terrible. Only five people were in front of him. After standing on line for a few minutes, Michael sat down with his cappuccino and let out a great sigh of relaxation. His body was heavy and tired. His eyes were starting to shut, so he quickly snapped up his head and took a big sip of his drink. The warm liquid felt soothing as it went down his throat. Michael got up and decided to walk while he had his coffee. He took his time walking back to campus and put his headphones in. He had subscribed to a new podcast a while back, so he decided to play that. He looked at his watch, 11:37 a.m. He wasn't too far from his next final, so he didn't have to rush.

He arrived at his next class with three minutes to spare. He walked inside, found a seat, and about ninety minutes later, he walked out. The final was uneventful, but inside, he had a mixture of relief and anticipation. Lucifer said he was going to come today, but when? His last final was at 2:15 p.m., so he decided to grab something to eat from the cafeteria and then go sit outside his last final to wait. At 2:10 p.m., the classroom door was unlocked, and Michael and others entered the room and found a seat.

Five minutes later, the professor emerged from the doorway and was already speaking as she walked toward the podium and placed down her exams. Students began to pass them back and get ready. Michael rubbed his eyes and then tilted his head from left to right in an effort to both energize himself and relieve some tension. He heard a cracking sound in his neck then stretched his arms up in the air to loosen his joints. As he rotated his wrists, he heard a crack emerge from his left elbow as well. He picked up his pencil, and then Michael began his last final exam. For a brief moment, it dawned upon him. His final, final. He smiled at the thought of it.

After about thirty minutes, Michael felt a slight pain in his abdomen. The pressure was building, and he knew that he had to go to the bathroom, but he decided to hold it. *Must have been the cappuccino*, he thought. At the rate he was going, he figured that he would be done with his exam in about twenty more minutes.

"Michael, go to the bathroom." Michael's head shot up and looked around the room. He knew deep down who the voice was but tried so hard in his mind to deny it to prove it wrong. "Go to the bathroom, Michael, before I send someone in there to get you." The voice echoed in his mind as the pressure grew stronger. He stood up and gathered his things then made his way down the aisle. The professor glanced over toward him with a look of inquiry. The professor tried to wave him toward her, but Michael paid no attention to her and just kept walking.

"Young man, where are you going?" she asked. "You cannot get up and leave during a final exam. It is against the rules." She watched as Michael just kept walking. She started again, "If you leave, I cannot let you back in."

Michael felt the pain get stronger and sharper, causing him to buckle a little from it. He arrived at the bathroom door and shouldered his way through. He began to walk down the hall with slow, nervous steps. The pressure continued to build so much that the pain forced him to walk faster. He rounded the corner and made his way into the bathroom. He moved quickly over to the sink, placed his hands on either side of the basin, and hung his head low. He began to spit into the sink and let out long, exhausting breaths. He felt like he has had a heavy night of drinking. Saliva was building up in his mouth like he was going to be sick. He turned on the faucet and took a couple sips of water. The pressure in his abdomen began to subside. Then he heard Lucifer's voice.

"Michael, what took you so long?"

Michael spat once more before responding, "What do you want?" Michael knew what Lucifer wanted.

"Michael, you know why I am here. It's time." Michael raised his head and stared into the mirror with a look of defeated frustration. "What's wrong? You seem displeased that I am here." The sarcastic sound in his voice made Michael angry, but his anger was hidden behind the resonating pain that hadn't completely left his body just yet.

"Fuck you!" Michael spat into the sink again. It pleased him slightly that doing so was in a way a symbolic gesture toward Lucifer about his feelings of this moment.

"Tsk tsk. Anger will get you nowhere. Now you have two choices here, Michael. You can come willingly or I will send someone in there to get you."

"Go where exactly?" Michael asked.

"To hell, of course."

Michael took a step back from the sink. "Wait…what? No way! There is no way I am coming with you to—" An immense pain began to grow inside his head, and his knees buckled, but he caught himself on the sink basin. He squeezed his eyes shut in an effort to dull the pain. Lucifer continued.

"Look, Michael, I really don't have time for this. You started this, and you are going to help finish it. Now which is it? Come willingly or be taken against your will?"

Michael envisioned some creature appearing out of nowhere and grabbing him, dragging him kicking and screaming out of the bathroom. His heart was pounding so loud that he almost couldn't hear the sounds of the room around him. He closed his eyes, and the words slipped out of his mouth as he heard himself say, "I will come."

Michael opened his eyes, and he was no longer in the bathroom. He felt his heart jump when he realized that he was standing in what could only be hell. He looked around and took in the surroundings. It wasn't exactly what he had envisioned as he expected fire and brimstone with an orange sky and fire everywhere. It looked like a valley that had been decimated by some great war. He scanned the terrain and couldn't see any sort of vegetation. It was a lifeless valley filled with dirt and dead tree limbs, some of which were still standing. He saw some fires burning but off in the distance in various spots across the terrain. They reminded him of piles of garbage or wood being burned, but they were not close enough for him to make out what was actually burning in the piles. The air there did feel hot though. Even the wind that blew was hot as if someone was holding a hair dryer toward him.

Off in the distance, Michael saw a bridge. He took a few steps toward it to try and make it out a bit more clearly. Then he was startled as he felt a large hand on his shoulder. He turned suddenly and stood in fear as a demon that must have stood well over eight feet tall was pointing toward the bridge. Michael couldn't move as he was fixated on the demon's empty-looking eyes and dry, rough skin. He noticed that its mouth was deformed and filled with jagged, pointy teeth, and its chin protruded out more than normal. Its skin was covered in black soot. Michael then noticed that the demon had hair braided around his forearms like they were bangles. Then the demon looked down at Michael once more, back at the bridge, and then grunted while shoving Michael toward the bridge.

Michael began to walk forward toward the bridge. He looked back, and the demon who had shoved him was already walking the other way. Michael continued to make his way toward the bridge. He saw people off in the distance being dragged by strange-looking figures. He heard the people scream-ing and begging as they tried to pull away but to no avail, they were being taken. To where, Michael did not even want to envi-sion. It reminded him of the visions Orrix had showed him, but he sensed the anguish and fear coming from the people was much greater. He continued onward, and then he arrived on the bridge. The bridge seemed over fifty feet wide and must have stretched on for a least a mile. At the foot of the bridge where Michael was approaching was a figure standing with his back to him. As he walked closer, Michael could see it was a man with blond hair. He did not have a top on, and his skin was pale. Michael looked closer and noticed that his back bore two symmetrical scars on either shoulder blade. Then the figure spoke.

"Welcome to hell, Michael."

Michael's eyes opened wide. "Lucifer."

Lucifer turned to face him and saw Michael just staring. "So, Michael, am I what you imagined?" he asked.

Michael stood with his mouth open as he looked over Lucifer. Lucifer stood maybe as tall as Michael did, about six feet tall. His blond hair hung down in his face just above his eyes. Michael had been expecting the classic devil character, red skin, black hair, but he looked practically human. His torso had a scar just below the center of his chest, and he held a sword in his right hand.

"I... I...you look human," Michael said.

Lucifer was expressionless. "Yes, I know."

Michael looked around. "Where are we? Is this hell?

"It's the bridge to hell. There are many circles here, and we are at the entrance. If Orrix wants in, he must come this way, and we will be waiting." He walked closer to Michael. "Now, Michael, I am going to get straight to the point here because we don't have any time. I am going to need your help in this matter, and when that is done, you will leave this place."

Michael felt himself straighten up. "What do I have to do?" he asked.

"Will you help? Yes or no."

Michael looked around at his surroundings. "Yes. Anything to get out of here. So, what is it? What do I have to do?"

Lucifer smiled. "Splendid. You will know when the time is right, trust me. So, are you ready?"

Michael shrugged his shoulders. "Ready for what?"

"The end. It's coming near."

Suddenly, Michael heard heavy breathing behind him. He turned and jumped a little as he saw just where the breathing was coming from. He was shocked to see a wave of creatures standing behind him. It was hard for him to make out just how many there were, but all of them seemed ready for battle. Almost all the creatures that he could see were holding weapons like swords, pikes, axes, and other large blunt objects adorned with rusted metals. Many of them wore very little clothing while others were dressed in various degrees of battle armor. Michael saw how some of the creatures had looked like your classic demons from films he had seen. Creatures with orc-like faces of which some had horns or tusks or both, and many of them had reddish skin while some others looked gray. Many of the other creatures had no horns and looked more reptilian and even a few looked insect-like. One such creature had damaged wings that reminded Michael of dragonfly wings. He focused on one demon-looking creature in particular who had armor, which looked to be a combination of leather, bone, and metal. Michael noticed the adornments on the shoulder armor; they were white feathers. He had wondered if those had been taken from angels.

Then a huge flash of light appeared toward the far end of the bridge. Michael watched as a man came walking out of the light with what seemed to be about twenty people walking behind him. Deep down, Michael knew that it was Orrix. Michael felt at ease knowing that based on what he could see, Orrix was heavily outnumbered. Then Michael remembered what Lucifer had said that Orrix and his spawn would be very formidable. Michael looked back toward Orrix and saw that he and his followers had started to run toward them and were moving at great speed. Michael looked over at Lucifer, and he was also adorned in armor now. His armor was gold, and it had white details which were smeared with more of the black soot he saw on other demons.

Lucifer raised his sword into the air and began to yell out, "Forward!"

At that moment, Michael was shoved aside as the creatures ran toward Orrix to intercept him. Michael lay on the ground frozen in a mixture of fear and horror as he watched the two sides meet toward the middle of the bridge head on. Lucifer stood by and watched also as the creatures he had summoned ran toward the oncoming foes. One wave stayed behind and stood waiting at the ready. Michael was surprised because as far as he could tell, there were just as many there now than seem to have headed out to the fight moments ago. Four of the creatures that headed toward Orrix did so with weapons raised when Orrix stopped running and stood still as the creatures continued to run at him.

One creature neared and took a swing at Orrix with a large battle-ax. Orrix moved quickly behind the creature and struck it in the back. The creature slumped over as Michael saw Orrix's arm disappear into the creature's back. He removed his hand, and the creature fell. Orrix quickly picked up the creature's ax and hurled it at the other three who were running toward him. The ax whirled through the air on a horizontal path toward the remaining three creatures. It struck two of them, and they dropped to the ground as the third creature continued toward Orrix. As with the first creature, Orrix quickly dispatched the last in the group and then continued forward.

Michael continued to look on as he saw more of Lucifer's demons fighting Orrix's followers. Lucifer's demons were being torn apart. Michael gagged as he saw the creature's limbs flying in the air as the vampiric demons ripped through them. Blood spilled down onto the bridge as the vampires moved forward. Michael sat up and moved closer toward Lucifer as if he was a shield that if Michael had just gotten behind, he would be protected. Then Michael watched as he saw some of Orrix followers beginning to fall. One creature with a double-ended sword decapitated one of the vampires while a second creature stabbed the vampire straight through the heart. The vampire immediately fell to bridge in a pile of dust. Michael watched as he saw Orrix's numbers starting to thin, but in Michael's estimation, Orrix's followers still seemed to be winning as Lucifer's army was thinning as well, and more of his second wave started to move toward the fray.

Many of Lucifer's creatures seemed to turn and run in a moment of fearful recognition of exactly who they were fighting against. Filled with anger, Lucifer moved forward and struck down those who tried to run. Michael rose to his knees and continued to watch as Lucifer continued to move forward, striking down not only the vampires coming toward him but the demons trying to run as well. Lucifer moved with speed that matched or quite possibly exceeded the speed of which Orrix was moving. Orrix was off to the far right of the bridge, but upon seeing Lucifer, he tried to make his way toward him. He moved quickly and swung wildly at the creatures in his path as if trying to carve a direct path to Lucifer. The ratio between the two sides was rapidly becoming even.

When it came down to handful of creatures and followers left, Lucifer stopped and let out a great yell as he said, "Enough! I command thee, all spawn of Lucifer!" Lucifer used his sword to cut open his hand and then flicked his hand out in front of him to spray his black blood onto the ground. "I command reclamation!" He then thrust his sword into the ground on the bridge. There was a great rumbling, and then the rest of the creatures and followers vanished. Now there was nothing but a dark mist that rose upward from the bridge. Michael stood there in total shock. Even Orrix seemed to be in shock. Orrix picked up a nearby sword and quickly charged at Lucifer with that sword raised, and they began to fight. Despite his fear, Michael began to move closer to see what was going on more clearly.

Lucifer moved quickly to the left of Orrix and blocked his incoming attacks. "You're finished, Orrix," he said. "I have come to finish what I should have done when I purged you and your kind."

Orrix continued to dodge Lucifer's attacks as well then responded, "You will not succeed. Hell is mine now, and your reign is over. The allegiance of the legions of hell will belong to me now. Even your kings will bow to me."

Michael watched as they continued to fight, moving all over the bridge. The echoing sounds of metal rang through Michael's ears. He was very close to them now. Orrix let out a loud sound of pain as Lucifer kicked him toward the edge of the bridge. As Lucifer charged, Orrix moved left and dodged his attack while quickly striking Lucifer hard in the back with the bottom of his sword's hilt. Orrix turned quickly to face him, and they continued. Their swords began to spark from the clangor they made. It was then that Orrix swung at Lucifer and struck his sword and must have hit it in the right spot as Lucifer's hand lost its hold on the sword, and it flew off the bridge. Orrix smiled while pointing his sword at Lucifer and began to walk toward him.

"Hell is mine now," Orrix said. "Tell me, how does it feel to be beaten by one of your own? All those years of serving you, for what? To be betrayed by the words of some imp. I was always loyal to you. Always! I would have conquered the world for you! My creator. My master! You who gave me this existence. This power. You cry reclamation, well now it is I who demand reclamation. I reclaim that which you have taken from me, and I claim all that is yours!" Orrix lurched forward and kicked Lucifer square in the chest. Lucifer fell and was now on his back crawling away while whispering something that Michael couldn't hear clearly. "Now that I have you, you have nothing to do but, what, pray? Well if you're praying to your creator, God won't help you. You made sure of that." Orrix raised his sword to strike when Lucifer raised his hand as if to block the strike and spoke.

"Stop!" Lucifer's voiced echoed all around.

Orrix stood frozen in place with a look of disbelief on his face as Lucifer started to stand. "What have you done?" Orrix asked.

"I stopped you. In the most literal sense of the word too."

Orrix was trying and failing to move. "How did you—"

"Do this?" Lucifer interjected. "I couldn't just do this right away you see. The power that I needed to do this requires sacrifice, blood, hence the battle. I needed time to conjure the spell and draw the power needed to not only reclaim your, well, my spawn, but also to stop you. While you may have grown stronger in battle than me, Orrix, I understand the dark arts more than you do. After all, I helped write most of them." Lucifer was face-to-face with Orrix now. "I made you, and I can unmake you, and that is exactly what I plan on doing! Michael, come here!" Michael began to walk closer to them when he stopped. "It's okay, he won't hurt you." Lucifer said reassuringly.

Michael stood and stared at Orrix as he stood there motionless and helpless. Orrix looked over at Michael. "You! What are you doing here? Why is he here?"

"He came of his own free will," Lucifer said.

Orrix was starting to struggle then looked at Michael. "You fool!" Then Orrix was free. He struck at Michael, who backpedaled and fell down. Lucifer backed away in surprise as well as his eyes opened wide.

"This can't be!" Lucifer said, amazed.

"Well, believe it, Lucifer. I have grown stronger than you know, and no one is going to stop me! Not you! And especially not him!" Orrix insisted.

"But you are forgetting something," Lucifer said.

"And what is that?" Orrix asked.

"Michael." Lucifer pointed at him.

Orrix looked at Lucifer then at Michael quizzically. "What about Michael?"

"You involved an innocent to gain what you needed," Lucifer said.

Orrix again stared quizzically at Lucifer, but for only a moment. "Yes, and I used him to get to the Matheson descendant. That isn't against the rules, he had a choice. He chose to do what I asked him. Therefore, his involvement was purely voluntary."

Lucifer smiled. "Exactly."

Orrix stared at Lucifer with hesitation and confusion. "What are you plotting?"

"Why, your painful demise, of course. This plot has run its course, and your time is over."

Just then, a brilliant light appeared behind Orrix, and standing just inside was a figure cloaked in darkness. Orrix faced the figure and then stepped backward as a look of fear overcame him. "No. No. *No!* This can't be. Why are you here?" The figure came forward through the portal, and as Michael made visual contact with it, his nose began to bleed and head began to pound. His body was now weak and throbbing with pain in every muscle. Lucifer stepped forward and grabbed Orrix by the wrist and forced him to drop his sword. Orrix turned to face him. The rage and hatred that was there a moment ago was now gone. All that remained was a mixed expression of regret and fear.

Orrix looked into Lucifer's eyes with inquiry then spoke softly, "Why has he come for me?"

"Well, he hasn't really *come* for you. He is merely assisting in this. You see, I needed someone to be able to take you through the gateway. I knew I couldn't get you to surrender or go of your own free will, so I asked for a favor. After all, death and I share mutual interests at times." Orrix began to struggle, and then Michael heard a voice in his head. It was Lucifer. "Run toward him, Michael." The voice echoed over and over. "Run toward him, Michael. Push him back into the gateway while I keep him distracted. Together we will end this." Michael was scared and sweating. "Do it, Michael! Do it, and then you can leave this place. I promise you, but you must do it now!"

Orrix continued to speak, "Back to purgatory? And what exactly do you think you are going to do?" Orrix began to struggle with Lucifer when Michael stood up and began to run toward Orrix.

"Well you see, Orrix, it isn't what I am going to do."

Just then, Michael collided with Orrix. Michael began to push him as hard and as fast as he could. His feet dug into the ground, and he inched his way against Orrix's resistance and tried to move him closer and closer to the portal. Lucifer was also pushing against him now. Orrix struggled furiously against the two of them.

"No! I will not go back!" Orrix insisted.

Lucifer responded, "Go back? You're not going back. You're going to the ninth circle in the fourth round."

Orrix screamed in anger which was met by cries of anger and hatred emanating from Michael as he continued to push Orrix toward the strange portal. Those cries of rage fueled him against the awesome energy that pulsed from Orrix. It seemed as if Orrix was beginning to get free from Lucifer and Michael. That was when the dark figure came up from the behind and grabbed Orrix and pulled him into the portal.

Orrix was stuck inside now. He regained his balance and ran toward both Michael and Lucifer, but he collided with an invisible barrier. He began to beat and pound his fists against what seemed like an invisible wall between both Lucifer and Michael. Orrix began to speak, "Lucifer! *Lucifer*! You devious fiend! I am going to get you. Hell will be mine! Revenge will be mine! I will make you suffer as I have suffered! I swear it!"

Lucifer stepped closer to the portal. "You'll never leave the ninth circle, Orrix. I'll make sure you suffer there for your treachery. Then after a time of my choosing, just when you are at your weakest, I will come to you and I will destroy you." Lucifer raised his hand. "Take him."

Then more figures cloaked in black appeared inside of the portal as they slithered left and right toward Orrix who swung violently at them to try and ward them off, but they grabbed him and began to carry him off. His anger-filled yells were still heard as he disappeared from view of Michael and Lucifer. Michael watched as the portal remained hanging in the air. Then it was silent. Even the previous noises that filled the environment seemed to have dissipated. It was just Lucifer and Michael now. Lucifer hung his head then spoke.

"Poor, Orrix. It's a pity really. Such power…gone to waste."

Michael steeped back toward the edge of the bridge and leaned against the stone side as he wiped the mixture of tears and sweat from his face and tried to regain his breath. He felt the grain of the dirt rubbing against his hot skin and seemed to find relief in that mild discomfort.

Lucifer approached him. "Well, done Michael."

Michael hesitated before he spoke as he cleared his throat, "Good thing you helped. I would have never gotten him in there on my own."

"I know, I needed your help too. He would never have suspected that you would have stood up to him."

Michael straightened up and cleared his throat once more. "So, that's it, right? My part is done. A deal is a deal. When can I leave?"

Lucifer looked over at Michael then back toward the portal. "Right, a promise is a promise." Lucifer raised his hand then paused. "Take him." The black figure suddenly reappeared and moved toward Michael then grabbed him by the arms.

"Wait! What-what are you doing?" Michael asked urgently. "You said I'd be finished and that I could go home. You said I could go home! You can't do this!" Michael was trying to fight free as he was being dragged toward the portal. His tears raced down his face and slammed against the dirt-covered bridge. His heels were now digging into the bridge as he was being dragged. "God, no, please! You can't do this! We had a deal! You can't!"

Lucifer was facing him now. "Well, you are partially right, Michael. Yes, your role in this is finished, but I never said you could go home. I simply said you could leave this place. I never said where you would be going."

Just then, Michael remembered what Lucifer said to Orrix about using Michael for his ends. "But wait, you can't use an innocent to help you. I'm an innocent! You can't do this!"

"Oh, that? I lied. I merely brought up that point to try and stall while your Cimmerian escort here came to claim the both of you. After all, you came willingly to hell, which makes you mine to do with as I please. Orrix was right, you are a fool, and I cannot think of a better solution then for the person who started this whole mess to spend the rest of eternity with the person whom he betrayed. Oh, how I think you will enjoy the ninth circle, Michael. Just wait until Orrix sees you. What things he must have to say."

Michael continued to struggle as his screams for mercy and help began to fade in the distance as he was being dragged through the portal.

"What can I say, Michael? You were weak and far too trusting, and now you share a fate similar to that of Orrix...and of me." Lucifer watched as the portal closed. "We are the damned, and we are the condemned."

ABOUT THE AUTHOR

 Jesse Rosenbaum grew up in Green Brook, New Jersey, and is now living in Vero Beach, Florida, with his family. He is an author of stories for both page and screen. He used to write for the Audio Disclosure music review website and podcast.

He is an avid reader of fiction, with a love for the horror, mystery, science fiction, and thriller genres but doesn't limit himself to those genres. That love extends to other creative mediums like comic books, movies, and TV shows in the same genres. Jesse's other passions are cooking, martial arts, music, and video games.

You can learn more about Jesse by visiting his Facebook page, website or by e-mailing him.

https://www.facebook.com/literallyjesse
https://literallyjesse.wordpress.com
literallyjesse@icloud.com